Treachery And Spells

Mary Catelli

Published by Wizard's Wood Press, 2016.

TREACHERY AND SPELLS

First edition. May 8, 2016.

Written by Mary Catelli.

The Witch-Child and the Scarlet Fleet

Sullen gray beneath the leaden sky, the sea swells rolled toward the distant shore. One uncommonly bold flying fish broke the surface, but only one, and no gulls soared. Neither fish nor bird wanted to go near the Scarlet Fleet's port.

No more than he did, thought Alik sourly, and sailed closer. The horizon showed no sign of the port. Even the cliffs were only a dark line on the horizon. They had hours of this yet.

The sail—drab, off-white, brighter than the seascape—swelled from his witch-wind and bore them on. And on. Other pirate strongholds lay near the ship routes they preyed on, but not the Scarlet Fleet, not so long as Habrec the Witch-Prince led them, and bewitched their ships to go wherever he pleased.

"We should have gone the way you came," said Constantine, abruptly, behind him.

The wind tugged at Alik's hair. For a moment, he pondered. Set the boat against the waves the right way, and turn the wind, and he could pitch Constantine overboard. Turning the wind again would ensure that Constantine could not get back aboard before he drowned. Then Alik, alone, could sail off and ignore both the king and the Scarlet Fleet.

Habrec would approve, of the death at any rate. He would have earned his noose, even if the king thought he had perished on the way to the stronghold with Constantine.

Alik turned to face the knight: dark, built like a bear, and glowering at Alik with amber eyes. Hellfire eyes, thought Alik, glaring back. Constantine's gaze shifted sideways as if he eyed at Alik's hair—that moon-blond, witch-child hair—as if he were surprised, and annoyed, that Alik had not dyed it while aboard the boat.

"Couldn't," said Alik. Maybe he would have brought them that way if he could, and maybe not—he sailed at the king's command, not of his own will—but it did not matter. They did not sail on a witch-ship like the Red Hawk.

"Did you try?" said Constantine. "Did they tell you you could not?"

As if the king would have let him take the Red Hawk—as if that would not reveal the falsity of their story.

"We should make haste as it is," said Constantine.

For this voyage to take a year and a day would not be a moment too long for Alik's taste. He turned his attention back to the sail before Constantine could bait him into more speech. If he had known how his moon-blond hair would mark him out in the kingdom, or that Egbert and the other fools on his crew, captured, would denounce the ingrate witch-child who had deserted them, he might never have had the courage to leave the Red Hawk.

But—his hands clenched into fists—that would not have mattered if the king had cared about his innocence, or his life, instead of ordering him back to the port.

A large swell bore the boat up higher. Alik adjusted the witch-wind, to fight less against the waves. He glanced at the cliffs again and thought them the worst possible distance. Far enough to brood before they arrived, but altogether too close.

"I can't speed the boat too swiftly," he said. "Even if I had the magics, I could not betray my knowledge to the pirates. It would imperil my ability to—serve the king."

Let Constantine find a bone to pick in that.

Constantine snorted. "They thought you powerful enough to be useful on a pirate ship."

"But not powerful enough that they feared making me angry." They had feared Hilarion like that—but only if they drove him to the wall, so that if he did not care whether he lived or died.

And they knew that Alik could not possibly be so powerful as Hilarion.

His mouth tightened. He had been powerful enough to deal with the pirates, if not the king. Even under Egbert, the Red Hawk might have escaped with the aid of his witchings and gone on a successful raid, to sail back here alive and in triumph, loot-laden. Alik drew his breath in and forced it out again. And having made him a pirate. Earned his noose, as the pirates would say—with admiration, no less—and force gin into his hands to drink to his success.

He eyed the shore again. Cliffs were coming clear, looking less like a line and more of a shape, and even this gray weather could not hide their color. He set the sail again, to bring them closer. This close, Constantine could tell if he dawdled.

And waiting would not make the port more pleasant.

Minutes later, he said, "We're nearly there."

Constantine grunted in surprise. "The cliffs—they're red?"

"As blood," said Alik. "Wasn't until last month that I saw cliffs come in any other color." At least, with his own eyes— images in a scrystone were so small as to look not quite real—but if they sailed for a year, a month, a week, and a day, he would feel not the least desire to tell Constantine his tales.

Constantine snorted. "Red as their sails. Dyed in blood, no doubt."

Alik opened his mouth to deny that—but could he? He eyed the rock again. That the cliffs were red was among his first memories, but the pirates had lived here for many a year before his birth.

The gap that marked the port came clear as a bit of grayness among the red. Alik steered the boat before he concluded—no, the pirates would brag of dyeing the cliffs red. Every night, in their cups, they would brag of it, not caring that every slave in earshot had heard it twenty times, and knew that the pirates who had done the deed had long died. The cliffs had been red before any pirates set up their port here.

He felt half surprised that the pirates did not brag of it anyway, but then, they could only if they had thought of it.

Constantine looked over the waters. Alik set his jaw and sent the boat toward the harbor. A dozen ships (the full dozen!) swung at anchor, their scarlet sails furled. Motley buildings, built of weathered wood, sprawled behind them. A fortress of stone with two towers loomed in the midst of the dingy huts. Nothing green, of course—nothing grew here. The red cliffs lurked behind, half-hidden by the buildings, crumbling in their own time.

That fortress would not loom in the royal city or any other port. He had seen that much. It would look like a commonplace warehouse. As for the rest, they would have clumped about the city gates where the poorest of the poor lived. Which described the slaves well enough, but the pirates lived no better.

He bent his attention to sailing onward, and watching for rocks. The witch-wind slowed under his hand, and the waters calmed as they sailed into the leeway side, and the harbor's shelter.

A shout sounded over the harbor; someone must have sighted them. Crowds gathered and gawked at the boat.

His shoulders set, Alik kept his gaze on the sail. He wished they could have arrived early, in the dawn grayness before the pirates roused from drunken slumbers, while slaves cherished their escape into sleep. If they had stolen ashore, Constantine could have hidden, and Alik claimed magical return. But that would have required another night on the high seas, and risking Constantine's realizing that—and it was too late now. The pirates had weather-witches enough to match against him.

He brought the boat to shore.

Constantine, wretched man, looked unperturbed by the swarm. Starvelings in filthy rags huddled in alleys and odd corners, but pirates and their favorites came as well, their finery ramshackle, ill-fitting, gaudy but clashing, none too clean—they pressed and pushed to stare better, and talked endlessly—though no one spoke to either of them, or loudly enough for them to hear clearly across the water.

And none of them started to fight. That would have been another chance to hide, fights never stayed small, even if he would have had to hide with Constantine.

The boat ground on the sand. Alik let the sails go slack and eased forward in the boat, to scramble out on the sands. Lighter by his weight, the boat rode up in the water, and he tugged it farther ashore. Constantine rose to climb out and heave the much lighter boat entirely ashore. No one, even a slave, came to help—of course.

In the crowd, his lip curled, another wind-witch watched him. Alik let his gaze go on. The wind-witches were no danger. None of them had bothered to learn more than the wind spells, and all had scorned him for his apprenticeship to Hilarion. Other wizards lived in the port—prisoners and slaves, whose spells were useful enough to keep them alive and not powerful enough to allow escape—those wizards might prove a danger to the two of them—but none of them appeared in the crowd.

And Maximus, the only powerful wizard among the pirates' ranks, no more appeared than Habrec himself did.

Constantine gave them all a contemptuous survey, as if wondering why he had chosen to come to this pitiful port.

Two pirates, enveloped by coats too large for them but of peacock-blue brocade, drew close enough to eye Constantine. They talked in low voices. Constantine straightened and stared back as if he had done a menial task in hopes of luring some pirate into treating him as a slave, so that he could teach him his lesson.

One weather-beaten pirate, with gray in his hair, waved at them, his hand already unsteady. His other hand held a bottle of gin, which, from how he hefted it, was already half empty.

"Ho. Come to join us? A short life and a merry one, I warrant you!"

Constantine, coldly, turned those amber eyes on him. The pirate gave him a grin that showed how few teeth he had left, and took another swig of gin before plopping down on the sand.

In the midst of the murmurs, a hoarse voice, barely human, rose. "The king. To the pirate king!"

The cry was taken up, echoing, resounding with cries of "The pirate king! The witch prince! Habrec!"

"Make haste, make haste," one wiry old pirate said. "He will be angry if we keep this from him."

Constantine managed to conceal his flinch well. The crowd surged forward and hustled Alik and Constantine along the stretch of packed red dirt, between decrepit hovels, that passed for a street. Constantine strode with contemptuous ease. Alik scrambled to keep up and thought, sourly, that Constantine had no difficulty passing for a man who wanted to be a pirate.

More and more bystanders pressed about them. Fewer slaves, but more pirates, gaudy in scarlet silk, or purple velvet, or brocade in intricate colors forming dragons or phoenixes.

Several slaves, in this alleyway or that, gaped at him. Some of them, he knew. Alik studied the dirt underfoot. His sober clothes bore neither silk nor velvet, but they were reasonably clean and intact—though he had once been one of their number.

All the more reason to make use of such escape as he had had. Alik straightened. Ahead stood the one well-built building in the port. Built of black stone, looming, the fortress had long made Alik wonder whether it had stood before Habrec sailed the Scarlet Fleet here. They walked toward it. Hilarion had not known of such a fortress or why anyone would build it, but Alik could not imagine either slothful pirates or driven slaves building so well—even if they had bothered to fetch the black stone.

Even in the cloudy day, the fortress cast a shadow over them, and the air, as still in a tomb, felt colder.

At the gates, Habrec's guards, perhaps the only souls in the camp with any discipline, eyed them and listened to the babble. Then they deigned to let in Alik and Constantine alone, under guard. A few blows from their spears' ends drove back any soul who tried to follow, even one claiming he had brought the twosome here and deserved reward.

Within a few steps, they left behind the light from the doorway.

Lowering though the clouds had been, they had let through more light than shone in here from the torches. Vaulted rooms and hallways rose into gloomy indistinctness. Under them, pirates and their captive playthings swarmed, filling the air with their din. Every now and again, a shrill laugh rose over all. Here silks and velvets bore embroidery in gold and jewels; whenever light struck them, they gleamed as brightly as the eyes, which watched like wolves awaiting the moment to strike.

Even these pirates pulled back, though, from the guards leading Alik and Constantine on and on, by a path Alik had walked only once before. That time, after Hilarion's death from fever but scarcely after his corpse was cold, the pirates had made him weather-witch aboard the Red Hawk.

The air still smelled of smoke, of fine vintages carelessly spilled, of blood. Many pirates had died here when a chance quarrel surged up, with those crowded about as likely to die as those quarreling.

Alik wondered why he had not felt, the last time, how surrounded by weapons he was. He had known they could strike him down on the moment, on a whim, but he had not felt the weapons so.

Constantine showed no sign of noticing.

Music drifted from ahead, muffled by the walls.

One pirate stood, for a minute, before their path. Alik
swallowed. This close to the throne room, the pirate had to be a
favored captain—and the woman on his arm, lacking the dull
eyes of most captives, looked avidly at them, as if she wondered
whether the captain's largesse extended to prisoners. Her dress
carried so much lace that Alik could not see the color of it, only
that much of the lace had been torn off other clothing to be
tacked on in a mismatched array.

He looked back as steadily as he could. Constantine, no
doubt, looked unworried and as if carved from granite—he did
not dare look aside to see that expression—and the guards moved
forward.

With a grunt, the captain turned aside. The woman's mouth
pursed, but she went with him. With them gone from the path,
the throne room lay clear, even here visible through the arch.
The guards moved them forward, inside.

Alik could not compare its size to that of the king's. This
windowless room, lit only by torches, was cavernous with
shadows. But though the walls lacked the pale smoothness of
marble, and the gleaming windows, the pirates gathered about in
finery more glittering than the king's courtiers had, however
often in mismatched colors or in disarray.

They left the center of throne room open, though.

The gilded throne, catching the torchlight, stood on a dais
opposite the door. On the black flagstones before it, a woman
danced. Her jewel-bright skirts flared like a flower's petals, in
shades of violet, sapphire, and scarlet.

And on the throne sat Habrec. The Witch-Prince, the Pirate
King, the master of the witchery that sent their ships across seas
without sailing on them and gave the Scarlet Fleet its power and
its terror-inspiring fame. Bigger than Constantine, lowering like
a bear, dark, bearing a sword that could easily slice Alik in half, he
watched the dancer through eyes narrowed to slits.

The guards stopped in the doorway, and not in order to send the two of them ahead.

Alik glanced sideways from the throne. The jester, simple, or frightened to simpleness by his capture, mumbled over his bauble. His bag of tricks lay at his feet with its welter of oddments, bearing slight enchantments to amuse. Alik's tongue touched his lips. He could not make out the musicians. Fortunate musicians.

Alik looked back to the throne. The jester would not perform until Habrec dealt with a stranger and a wayward wind-witch who arrived by boat. Though as the music went on, and on, Alik wondered whether that was because the dance would last long enough to unnerve them.

The woman swirled, colors flaring. Alik fought down fidgets but could not wrestle down his thoughts. They stood in a pirate stronghold, he had deserted a pirate ship, all its pirates had died on the gallows, Constantine was a knight in the king's service. . . .

Alik forced his breath in and out. Habrec was not some madman. All the captives had been captured in raids on towns and cities, or ships foolish enough to fight or flee. Merchant ships that cut their colors on the sight of a ship from the Scarlet Fleet lost only what the pirates craved from their cargo, not their passengers, not their sailors. Habrec, pragmatic soul, had enforced that rule with executions and liberated captives taken from ships, to preserve and keep strong the fleet, and it lasted so well that he had never had to either execute or liberate in Alik's lifetime.

But he remembered the tale of a ship that the pirates had thought carried gold. Finding only pale gray ingots, they had cursed them as tin and thrown overboard a king's ransom in silver.

A pirate bellowed for wine, and a slave scurried with the jug, to pour with her head bent low, trying to avoid notice.

He should stop acting as if he had not seen the throne room many times before, if only once by this route. Constantine had not shuddered—he glanced sideways and saw the tension in the knight. He glanced away before the knowledge could infect him with more terror.

The music stopped.

The woman sank in a curtsey deeper than any woman had given the king, glided off the floor, and sat in a corner, her eyes downcast.

For a long minute, Habrec did not stir, his gaze still on the floor where the dancer had stood. Then, he looked up. Slowly, his gaze crossed the distance between them. He looked over Constantine with a leisure that Constantine's stubborn expression did not perturb. Then his gaze settled on Alik as if eying every inch answered all his questions, and not one answer pleased him.

Finally, he looked at the guard. His voice was a thunderous growl. "There had better be a good reason for you intruding on—amusements not meant for your ilk."

"News from the Red Hawk, my lord," said the guard.

Habrec shook his head. "Not news. News only if that witch-child finds his tongue and tells the truth. I know I did not send some starched paladin with him. I wonder whether he really is old enough to win his noose."

Words surged to Alik's mouth. Even knowing Habrec baiting him, as he baited many another in this hall, he had to fight to hold them back. A pirate duel would end him. The king's plans could roll on without him; Constantine would not intervene on his behalf.

Habrec's lip curled. "A bookish little witch-child. I should have known Hilarion would make you as useless as he was."

Laughter prowled about the court.

Though Hilarion had taught Alik from every book he could lay his hands on—begged, borrowed, or lying about unheeded—

he had also taught him how to act in a pirate king's court, etiquette taught in no book. Habrec had given him no orders. Alik stood as still as he could.

"Come." Habrec straightened. Alik walked forward. Constantine calmly followed, as if the center of the throne room were not the hardest place to defend, and the best lit, leaving all his foes in shadow. The air, laden with the smell of smoke, stood perfectly still about him. Alik felt like a candle flame, tossed by drafts, unable to keep steady a moment, and in danger of being blown out.

Habrec drew his sword. It gleamed like ice as he brought it down, its tip pointing inches from Alik's feet.

"Speak, witch-child." His deep voice grew more menacing, like the advance of a towering thunderhead. "Tell me of the Red Hawk. Tell me of the ship I placed you on, to win your noose."

His court was, for once, silent. Not even the slave children's footfalls sounded. Alik felt as mute as any of them, but all was lost if he kept silent.

"It foundered, Your Majesty." With a little well-placed help from a little wind-witch—but Alik kept his voice level. "The captain and crew alike foundered it." True enough. If they had not insisted that wind-witchery do all the work, if they had acted as sailors, he would never have had his chance. At the time, he had grown dizzy with joy. "They were caught and hanged by the neck until dead. Their bodies still hang from the gallows."

Not even the last drew a murmur from the crowd.

"Waste of a good ship." Alik shrugged. "Should I have wasted a wind-witch, trying to rescue them? As if I could—I can not witch such an escape." He raised his head to meet Habrec's gaze. "But I escaped, with some aid, and brought a warrior to add to your numbers, one not so worthless as the crew of the Red Hawk." To add a traitor and spy to your numbers—but Habrec hardly desired his advice.

Habrec snorted. "Still the bookish little mouse that Hilarion taught." A low rumble of mirth came from the crowd. Habrec sat back. "But you have served me well enough."

It felt as if the flagstones had vanished underfoot. The room was silent again. Alik did not move; he did not breathe; he only waited for Habrec to spring his trap.

"Another task I have for you, since you serve me. Kill me this companion of yours."

Alik started and stared at Habrec. Even Habrec's presence could not hold back the guttural laughter, all about the room.

"Your Majesty, he helped me—"

Habrec sneered. "So he could become a pirate, not out of his tender heart. And you owe him for that? More than you owe the Witch Prince who holds the freedom of the seas for the Scarlet Fleet?" He lowered his voice. "The Witch Prince who gives you another chance to earn your noose, and win a short life but a merry one?"

He produced a knife like a conjuror's trick; one moment, it was just there, in his hand: a long jagged knife with, Alik guessed, a handle of bone.

He hurled it, and it clattered on the floor at Alik's feet.

Alik drew a deep breath. In, out. In, out. Then he knelt to take the knife up. The handle was, indeed, bone, and felt cool under his fingers.

A statue could not have stood more still than Constantine. From his face, he might have been struck deaf when Habrec spoke, and so be ignorant of the order. Until Alik, turning, met his hellfire eyes and saw the flicker of contempt in them. He thought—and King Petros would think—it was Alik's duty to kill him and preserve his ability to spy—as Habrec thought it was his duty to kill aboard the Red Hawk.

At the moment, if he had known a spell to blast every living thing in the world, he would have cast it.

With the knife in hand, he rose. A ball fell from the jester's hand, and Alik's eyes narrowed.

"So slow," drawled Habrec. "So reluctant."

"To botch it before the Pirate King?" said Alik, glad of an excuse to face the throne rather than Constantine. "A wind-witch is not a master of blades, and I should not leave him floundering in his own blood like a landed fish, so that another has to finish him off." He shrugged. He felt light-headed and wondered if he had gone mad. "Unless you gave me the knife as a sign I should witch him to death."

Habrec snorted as if conceding a point. "As if you could kill a man with light and wind, little witch-child—but you know enough of a blade."

Alik nodded. He noted in his mind where Constantine stood, a little behind him. "Quite enough. For this."

The knife flew through the air, before him. Roars of fury rose. Poison-green witchfire flared about Habrec, ready to ward the blade off.

The knife flashed past the throne, like a hawk seeing nothing but its prey, and tore into the jester's bag of tricks.

For a moment, in the startled silence, Alik thought it all in vain. He had missed any enchantment that would have mattered, and doomed them both.

Then the bag burst from the magics inside. Lights in gold and white and blue fountained out, drowning out the witchfire and filling the air to the roof with their brilliance. Even having turned his face away, Alik was blinded. But ready.

He surged back to Constantine. Grabbing his arm, he said, "With me."

Not a moment too soon. Uproar echoed throughout the hall, drowning anything he could say, but Alik drew Constantine off with him, to the wall behind the throne. Screams punctuated the clamor—screams, mostly, of "I'll kill him!" Alik fumbled with his free hand, knowing where it was but not where he was.

The wall yielded to emptiness, so abruptly that Alik staggered into it. Then he fled, giving his eyes, and Constantine's, no time to adjust to the gloom.

At least Constantine had followed without question. The pirates would rage to kill. Likely, they struck about the throne room already and killed some of their own number. Escape was possible only before the spells ended, and the pirates could see, and see how many they had killed, and swear revenge on him for that as well.

And Hilarion had made him memorize the way—

The window slits, high up on the way, gave him light enough for him to see his still too dark path, before he realized what his memory meant. He stopped.

Constantine bumped into him, hard enough to knock him a step forward. His words pushed out past his teeth, in a barely intelligible snarl. "What fool thing now, witch-child?"

The first place they would seek him was Hilarion's old hut. He forced his breath out. Constantine glared at him. No longer too surprised to do anything but obey, but he still did not know the ways. He had to use Alik as his guide, even if Alik did not know the ways perfectly.

Which, Alik thought, would be wise to keep from Constantine.

"This way," he said—down another slave corridor, which at least the pirates would not know. It led to a door strange to him. Opening it revealed a narrow passageway between ramshackle huts. Unlike the street, most huts lacked doors to it, and it was far narrower. He could not tell which one it was, but he would know soon enough.

Constantine eyed it and said nothing, but followed. After a minute, Alik held up his hand to stop him. Clamor burst out next to them, pirates swarming from the fortress and tumultuous noises reaching through the thin walls. He could hear nothing clearly of what they said, but he could almost see the torches and weapons.

They had feared to make Hilarion desperate, had even let him die of his illness before they claimed his apprentice. They should have feared the same of him. Though—Alik's mouth twitched— none of them perhaps had realized that it would make him desperate, that order.

Hilarion would have approved, he thought, despite the danger.

He glanced sideways. Constantine at least had the wit to stand still despite the ruckus.

Someone bellowed, demanding to know what was going on. The footsteps did not move as far as the shouting rose. Jeers rose, that only fools would let captives escape, and then the sound of blows. Even a Pirate-King could bring only so much order to pirates. Smiling a little, Alik hurried along again, while the hunt turned into a brawl.

The slave alleyways interlaced throughout the huts and hovels of the port, with walls to shield them from the pirates. He scurried through them like a pale little mouse, eying the path ahead. The slaves had to be cowering away from the rage, but the corridors had gaps, so that slaves about their tasks could slip in and out, and there they could be seen. Each time he came to one, they flitted across with extra care, and Alik breathed a sigh of relief every time they were not seen. After half a dozen, he thought the pirates must have gone to see the ruckus. They had best use the time wisely, before Habrec enforced his will—the noise of the shouting and fighting was not far behind them—but Constantine, even if a large, dark mouse, was as silent as he was. Alik led on.

One relieved moment, he realized for certain where he was, and started their path, out of the central buildings, toward the half-empty ones. Constantine eyed the tumble-down shacks but said nothing. Alik kept an ear cocked to the ruckus. The noise did not seem to spread—it even seemed to die down—but the pirates would be quieter as they stopped fighting and started searching. He could not keep his breath from coming light and fast. If he escaped this port alive, he would delight in having defied Habrec as no one else had ever dared.

If.

Finally, they reached a plunder house. Not where the pirates stored food or rope or water, or anything else useful, but fripperies that had caught no pirate's fancy, and that they had not needed to trade. Alik slid through the door.

Only the daylight that slithered through cracks where its boards were ill fit together gave the place any light, and sounds from outside were muffled. Dust like a veil of years lay over every crate and bale. Pirates had made slaves build new shelters for their loot, and slaves had not raided for anything here.

Alik sighed, turning his face away. Useless enough that they might hide safely here.

Constantine's hands clamped around his throat, and he squeaked—the noise cut off as Constantine's grip tightened.

In a rage-laden growl, Constantine said, "*What* did you—" The words cut off as if Constantine was being choked, and Alik, futilely, kicked. He had no chance of landing a good blow, but Constantine hurled him down, knocking him against a crate.

Alik lay against it, breathing hard. He would have bruises where he struck the wood as well as on his throat. If, that was, Constantine did not finish what he had begun.

Constantine stood in the largest clear space on the floor, breathing hard, engulfed in shadow. Alik could not see his face in the gloom, but his hands formed fists and released them, again and again, and he fought to steady his breath.

Finally he spoke, forcing out every word. "What fool thing did you think you were doing?"

Alik drew a deep breath. "Saving your life."

"So it means nothing to you," said Constantine. "The dead children—the ruination—the horrors they inflict when next they assail a city—you wandered through a city and saw all that would die when they attack—"

Alik let his breath out. As if Constantine's purpose here were not to keep him as the king's spy.

"Finish it, then," he said, curtly. "No matter you might, with my aid, still carry out the king's command." He turned his back to Constantine and pushed off the ground—his arms ached—to stare into the massed crates. And wait.

His heart beat out the moments too fast for him to judge time by them. And how long should he wait? They could not stand here forever, but Constantine would not speak.

Finally, he looked over his shoulder. Constantine glared so banefully at him that Alik thought only the lack of words poisonous enough kept him silent.

Constantine's gaze shifted up to meet Alik's. He grated out each word. "You didn't even know those spells would work like that."

"Where did you imagine the jester got them?" said Alik.

Constantine's voice softened not at all. "What do you intend to do now?"

Alik swallowed, making the bruises ache. "Sneak. The port has a maze of alleys all about, so slaves can sneak, unnoticed."

Constantine snorted. "I wouldn't think pirates would care."

"They don't like the riff-raff getting underfoot."

Constantine's hand swept the air, dismissing. "Enough to build these ways?"

"Pirates?" said Alik. "Build? Anything? Stab a slave for a glance at a favorite, or no reason at all, yes, but *build*?" He looked about. "Or even store things away—I doubt any pirate can tell what clothes they have here." He glanced at Constantine. He had, after all, started this to save Constantine's life; he might as well carry on. "You'll have to skulk. Unless you want to try to swagger off as a pirate. Or pass as ill."

Constantine snorted. "*Ill.*"

Alik tilted back his head to meet his gaze. "I dare say Rosalba—she's a herbwoman—could whip up a posset to have you coughing and feeble, if you want the risk of dying for their sport. As you stand now, when any pirate sees you—a man like you is a pirate, or kept in chains if he's skilled enough to keep alive—and you're no blacksmith, or rope-maker, or wizard, or doctor."

"You should have thought that before you started this." Constantine's lip curled. "I suppose they still think you a child."

"They're like you. I'm man enough to sail as a pirate, and man enough to hang for it. But other than that—" Alik turned to the crates. Not, of course, tightly nailed up. Pirates had torn them open to see the loot. Even when nails had been restored, the planks were loose, and he could strew the clothes he did not need all about.

"They leave these things hanging about?" said Constantine, his lip curling. "So much for a short life and a merry one—they could trade this loot for more revelry."

"Point of pride," said Alik, prying open another crate. "Sometimes they trade, if they are short on rope or the like, but they say that with the Witch-Prince's magic sending them to where they can strike best—" The plank leapt free, making him stagger. "—they can hardly *need* to sell it." He tossed the plank aside. "A few more raids would cover it. They have to direct them, sometimes, to get food and water, and even—" He seized another plank. "Even raid land for food. But *trade*? No, they leave the loot for foolish slaves if they want it."

It took some minutes to find the best crate, but that one revealed clothing too drab to catch the pirates' gaze. Alik sorted out some shabby, ill-fitting clothes, dragging it out to the best light to be sure of the colors. It would not offend the pirates, prone to stabbing slaves for taking clothes the pirates had not wanted, but it was neither tattered nor stained with reddish dust. Yet. He doubted the dust would take an hour, and they could never be clearly seen. Pirates would see who they were before they missed the tatters.

He carefully pulled out a hood for himself. Dingy blue, but the color hardly mattered. He could not let a pirate see his eyes, either, but the hair they could see from a distance, and it would be as distinctive and betraying here as in the kingdom.

About changing, at least, Constantine did not argue. As he straightened his new ash-brown tunic, he said, "How safe are we in the slave passages?"

"Slaves may rat us out." Alik transferred his own knife to the new clothing. "Not many. Not from loyalty, but only a fool would expect a reward." His mouth twisted. "Still, we are not short on fools. And some will be just too afraid to not tell, unless they fear us more."

"Domenic," said Constantine, without looking at Alik. "Domenic may live yet—not having been shackled to such *help* as you." He swept a loose mantle about himself. It at least swathed if it did not hide his weaponry. It might work at a distance.

Alik nodded and turned to leave. With only one doorway, this building was no place to be caught. Even a wizard could see that. His mouth set. And they did have to find Domenic, and act against the pirates, who would hunt them down in time.

He still did not know how he managed to walk briskly down the corridors again, until they came within earshot, and walked as softly as little mice again.

Voices were still clamorous, outside, but nowhere near as loud as before. By one doorway, making out laughter, Alik stopped and held out his hand, flat, before Constantine. They stood there, Alik scarcely breathing.

The pirates roared with mirth over what fools the captains looked like, running all about after Alik vanished—carried himself off to the kingdom again, he gave it away when he talked about escape spells—nah, if Hilarion could have taught him he would have escaped himself—but Alik could have stolen a spell book for his studies since then, it took him long enough to return—and Alik crept onward, despite the risk, knowing the pirates would not leave.

The pirates argued on, whether he had turned invisible and sat in the great hall, pilfering jewels and fine wine. That, they thought most likely. Why else would he have returned?

The voices faded behind, and Alik's mouth twisted. No mention of Constantine—Alik wondered whether they knew he existed. Rumor could have left him out as too dull to discuss.

He ducked into a roofed alley. From the gaps in the wall, light splattered on other side, beige spots on dull brown wood, like a dreary, captive wildcat.

"Spy holes," said Alik, softly. "We're on a hillside—you can see the square below."

Constantine eyed the holes. And why not? thought Alik. The biggest square, where they divided loot, and fought duels, and drank to drunken slumber—where was more likely to hold Domenic?

Outside, the clouds had thinned enough to show watery sunlight. An enormous pile of wood sat in the square. Pirates gathered around, glancing often at a doorway, and some talked of how long it would take.

"Ho!" someone shouted. Pirates—Alik scowled, but he could clearly see them—pirates themselves lugged their burden, with others cheering their efforts on.

A boat, Alik realized.

Not just any old boat, but the one he and Constantine had arrived on. The pirates hefted it onto the bonfire wood to merry cheers.

Alik forced his breath in and out. It was, indeed, any old boat, chosen for its ordinariness. The magic to bring them here had been Alik's own, the pirates had boats like it, boats that the two of them could steal in the end, but Alik felt like a prisoner seeing the key to his cell being destroyed.

A pirate brought the burning torch to the wood. For a moment, smoke emerged, and nothing more, as if the wood stifled the torch. Then flames leapt up and licked the driftwood. They blossomed orange, with shots of blue or purple running through them, and grew toward the boat. The fire crackled and sent fountains of sparks into the air.

Constantine's hand rested on his shoulder. "Best time to move. That will distract them."

Alik nodded, but said, "I can do better." He held out his hand and readied the spell. Nothing more than amusing trick, usually but—his eyes narrowed, as he invoked the words.

The flames on the boat shot up a pure snow-white. Alik took only a moment to relish the horrified expressions before he followed Constantine. They would take it for something in the driftwood, or the boat, but it would hold them.

Indeed, voices already demanded that some wizard explain what enchantment the boat had held. And why he had not seen it first.

The alleyway held rickety stairs, leading downward over a slope. Alik drew a deep breath. Here, the alleyways would be more heavily traveled; the one down the stairs was the worst, lying between the ale barrels and the pirates' revels. They needed every scrap of wariness they could muster.

Something flitted through the air—bird-like, glinting golden when stray light fell on it—and toward them. Alik's heart drummed almost before he realized what it was. He had only seen them once, he had been too young to understand much then, but the mere sight brought back terror and memories of sudden blood.

"Kill it?" whispered Constantine.

Alik nodded.

Constantine's sword whispered out. As the shape flew closer and grew more clearly hawk-like, he lunged. The sword bit between wing and body. The thing fell into a clutter of metallic feathers—all feathers, apparently, except for its sharp beak and claws, which twitched on the dusty floor.

Grim-faced, Constantine struck again. Feathers flew and lay still.

His mouth dry, his heart only slowly quieting, Alik dropped to one knee. The pirates might not chase them, but Habrec had others to aid him. A wizard like Hilarion might win some respect from pirates for fear of what he might do if desperate. A wizard like Maximus, who held respect and received his share of the loot, had to please the pirates to hold that place.

Alik poked through the ruined bird, and his back prickled with the knowledge that another bird could fly toward him at any time. Still—

His mouth dry, he said, "It's not very good. He has nothing of yours or mine to strengthen it." He swept up the shattered bits, to hide them. "But I know Maximus. He won't send only one, because he can send a whole cast of them. Force of numbers will take us down in time." He drew a deep breath and straightened before glancing about the ways, remembering. "We have to stop them at the source."

Constantine snorted. "You think Habrec won't notice the death of a pet wizard?"

"No. He wouldn't." Alik set out briskly, down a new corridor. "At most he would notice the lack of spells, and in his rage, he might learn of the death—but since we will not kill him, it does not matter."

At least, this path took them by uncommon ways, and they could move with haste.

Constantine strode after without more questions. He did not put up his sword. Another gleam in the dark shadows had him striking again. Alik gathered up the feathers—these ways were not so little used that they could leave a trail—and Constantine stood watch over him.

"How long?" he said, glowering, as Alik straightened. "Do we chase about this port for hours on end?"

"Not much farther," said Alik. Unable to take themselves off into towers, wizards lived at the edge of the port—though not so far off they had to fear escaped slaves. Which meant the two of them had nearly reached it.

He turned his gaze back on their path, and his eyes narrowed. Just as well. Maximus would have gone slowly at first, but the birds would multiply swiftly once he had refined the spell. After a moment, he ran. When Constantine smashed a third bird against the wall, Alik ran on without breaking stride. Cleaning up the bird later would have to be enough. They could not be caught standing over it.

The floor turned into a ledge, with a short stair leading down from it. Opposite stood a building—sturdier than a hut, with rooms and windows. Alik jumped. He landed, with a jolt, before an arched doorway, filled with shadow.

Not too many shadows—they did not hide the bowl, larger than a ship's wheel, glittering with a golden liquid that rose almost to its brim. Mist rose from it in pale coils, as if from the sea on a cool evening, but mist should not twist around, take on bird-like form and solidity, and dart toward them.

Constantine's sword flashed out, striking it down. Alik drew a deep breath and wove his sealing spell. Another hawk had almost formed as he reached the end. Two more were forming.

The last word slid out, and he squeaked, "Fall back!"

For a fearful moment, he thought Constantine would not listen. Then, he inched away, his gaze on the birds. They took on fuller form and snapped at the air with strong jaws. Alik's heart beat out the moments—

"Faster!" he said.

Constantine swore, but leapt back. His foot caught on the uneven floor, and he stumbled, falling to one knee. A golden hawk plunged to the attack. Alik's knife sliced through the air, pinning the creature to the wooden wall.

Behind it, a swarm of golden hawks splattered against the seal. They snapped and struggled but did not cry out. Alik's mouth twisted. Even Maximus, monumentally self-absorbed, would have had a hard time avoiding the racket if they screamed—no doubt the reason for their silence.

He let his breath out and rubbed the back of his neck. The other good fortune was that Maximus was too proud of his hawks, and too absorbed in his studies, to come and check.

Alik retrieved his knife. He hoped that there was not too much more luck ahead. If he exhausted his good fortune in the first hours in this port, he would die soon. They still faced the pirates, and whatever other witchery Maximus or some other wizard could cook up, and any runaway slaves sulking in shadows and stealing what they could.

He put up the knife. Not to mention that Constantine already had little inclination to listen to him. He collected the dead birds, and turned to climb the stairs. They still needed to gather the other one, and then it might be wiser to take a roundabout route to other places where they might glimpse Domenic—

"How long will *this* last?" Constantine's voice was heavy on the air.

Alik hesitated and racked his memories for how the moon had been when they set sail. The last measly scarp of a crescent— "Two days." He turned on the steps. "The *spell* would last much, much, much longer, but even Maximus will have to notice it when he leaves, at the first crescent. He'd hide in his hole forever, if he could but—" Alik shrugged. Maximus would come out to strengthen some spells, the price of Habrec's favor, but all

Constantine needed to know was the time. "In two days, we have time to do things."

Constantine snorted, putting up his sword, and walking toward the stairs. "We'll see. If Domenic has not done better than we have, we may do nothing."

Alik shrugged again. "We have to act quickly, whatever happens. Habrec will not keep the ships here forever."

That silenced Constantine.

Alik led the way back to the last bird, which he gathered up with care. He crouched over where it had laid a minute longer, considering which path to take now.

"We came that way," said Constantine, his voice harsh.

Alik straightened up. "Did you see Domenic in the crowds?"

After a moment, Constantine shook his head. "I looked," he admitted. His face was half shadowed.

The daylight was fading under clouds again, Alik noted; they would have to return to the torch-lit parts before they were lost in gloom.

"We will cast about for other places where they often gather. By routes that the slaves are less prone to take." He glanced at his hand. "We can throw these aside in a back corner where no one will look, while we are at it."

And I know the route better if we go another way. He tried to push that thought away—and then to distract himself by picking out the way and heading off.

Several huts stood to the side of Maximus's, farther apart than most. They crumbled into dust. No one wanted to move into a wizard's home after his death—even the wretched hut of a feeble wizard, who could not escape pirates and eked out a living with tricks for pirates and even slaves. Alik's brooding gaze moved over them. Maximus would say that they were even too feeble to win Habrec's regard. Alik's eyes narrowed; then, he had heard the tales of how Maximus had groveled and begged and promised anything for his position. Hilarion, he knew, had not.

His gaze moved ahead, as if drawn by a lodestone. His feet moved more slowly. He would hate seeing it, but by this path, he had to. His free hand clenched into a fist.

Hilarion's hut showed no outward signs of ruin, but its door swung open. He peeked inside. Enough gray daylight seeped in to show that the hut had been stripped bare, of everything from Hilarion's scrystone to the beds and cooking pots. His fist tightened. His mother's hut had been stripped at her death, he had been lucky that Hilarion had taken him in, but he had not seen this; they had snatched him to be a weather-witch almost before he finished burying Hilarion.

They would laugh and tell him to be grateful that they allowed the burial.

"That one's barely damaged," said Constantine. "Best place to hide the birds—"

"No," said Alik so abruptly that Constantine blinked. But he did not owe the knight an explanation of his life. "The next one will be better." He walked briskly to it and told himself that some foolish soul might hope that not everything of Hilarion's had vanished, and visit the hut. It took him only a minute to throw the feathers into a corner. He drew a deep breath and went to lead the way back into the heart of the port. Down dusty alleyways—he had lived in this red dust all his life, but now, after only weeks away, it bore down on him.

He let his breath out very slowly. He might escape it yet.

Down a few rows of huts, he hesitated, hearing footsteps ahead. He drew Constantine to a corner.

Constantine scowled. "This won't hide—"

Alik shook his head and gave him a sharp glance. And cast his spell. Shadows gathered round, making the very air murky. For them, thought Alik, nothing more than murk, but at least Constantine held his tongue.

The slave, a boy with a bruised face, scurried along without a glance at their corner.

Alik released the spell. "That only works for a place," he told Constantine. "And not well if we move, even in it."

Still scowling, Constantine nodded, and they stole along alleyways. Footsteps had them hid in odd corners, sometimes with shadows. Through spy holes, or the cracks that slipshod building had often left, they eyed the pirates as they fought and drank, and roared tales of real or imaginary fights and treasure hauls. Alik remembered the art of darting across streets where pirates fared without being noticed. Perhaps he was even too cautious there, but for now, at least, they had time for safety.

Perhaps. The endless array of pirates and slaves and favorites exhausted him. Could they search all the port in two days? Some pirates were new—some slave boys sent to earn their noose after he left, but others taken off ships, and he had no notion whether he could recognize this Dominic.

And it could happen that Dominic could not help them at all.

He trudged on. The passing of hours meant they could check every place twice, and still miss Dominic, what with all the movement among them. Even the gray daylight started to slacken as they searched on.

Then Constantine, peering from the shadows by a doorway, pointed. A man, as dark and bear-like as Constantine, leaned on a table over his ale. He sat back, unsteadily. His clothing looked drabber than most pirates', though he wore a sky-blue vest and a flame red sash across it. The colors clashed.

Another pirate shouted for Domenic to come. He lifted his head.

"Huh. I'll stay with—" He raised his mug. "Good ale."

Constantine's voice, low by his ears, said, "Wiser than you in evading what he does not wish to do."

Alik drew his breath in and forced it out again. Slugging Constantine would do him little injury and would draw eyes. Nevertheless, his fingers curled together, and then after he had forced them apart, curled again.

"How do we get about, behind him?" Constantine pointed at the wall behind Domenic.

Alik walked off, picking the way, wary of slaves bearing ale. The walls here were more ramshackle than usual, where slaves had need to spy; when he glanced out a crack between planks, Domenic no longer sat where he had. Alik swallowed but walked on, hoping for revelations.

"There you are." The voice was clear, sober, and recognizable. Alik stopped.

Without faltering, Constantine pushed by him and clapped Domenic on the shoulder. His voice was low but amused. "Amethyst still working well, I see."

Domenic nodded. Not so tall as Constantine, broader in the shoulder—plus the finery, which made it easy to distinguish.

"If," said Domenic, "we had aimed to cause uproar among the pirates, I would say you had succeeded beyond the king's dreams."

Constantine rolled his eyes. "There is no need to remind me. This, for my sins, is Alik."

Domenic inspected him. For a moment, Alik studied the beaten earth; then, feeling defiant, he straightened and met Domenic's gaze. Let Domenic see how moon-pale he was— down to the pale gray eyes, and the even paler eyelashes.

Domenic's eyes were dark, unreadable. After a minute, he snorted. "Watch how you stare—even in the slaves' alleys. I saw you."

Alik forced his breath out.

"Have you learned anything?" said Constantine.

Domenic nodded. "Habrec's going to raid another city. He's chosen a city, he's drawn up his orders—and not for a chest of medicines, this time."

Alik flinched. Neither knight seemed to notice.

"He's sealed them in the Tower of Winds. But I can't stagger there under the pretense of drunkenness. Even in the slaves' alleys." He snorted. "Especially in the slaves' alleys."

"I've been there," said Alik, surly. When Domenic looked at him, he glared back.

"What do you want?" said Domenic.

"To be very far from here. You know how I was sent." His eyes narrowed. "I am not here of my own will."

Domenic snorted again. "There is no place far enough for you to have no fear of the Scarlet Fleet."

"Am I the only person that's true for?"

Constantine, cutting in like a sword blow, said, "Does Habrec venture to the Tower of Winds by evening?"

Domenic scowled.

"No," said Alik. "Habrec doesn't get so drunk as the rest, but he spends the nights like any pirate." He glanced up, past the tower and the cliffs. The clouds had thinned farther, to show that the sky had turned flaming red and pink. About the port, pirates had lit torches, here and there. Orange light blazed on walls and cast dark shadows, but it would seep into the back alleys as they went. Enough to walk by, if they took care.

"We had best be off," said Constantine. "To find it in the hours before they start to rouse again in the morning—and *you* have to go back to drinking."

Domenic cocked an eyebrow but left. After a few strides, he staggered into the torchlight. Alik looked away. For all the books, for all the scenes Hilarion had shown him in his crystal, he had never seen knights as such actors—though if they acted well, he would not have known they were knights.

And Constantine's glare was no act.

Alik walked along the alleyway, pondering that both knights had offered to come here at the king's command. Though *they* had chosen the king's service.

After some minutes, with sounds fading behind them, Alik said, "We're taking the back route. It will be full night by the time we get there, but fewer slaves, that way."

Constantine muttered, "Some sense anyway."

How flattering, Alik thought, and prowled on. They circled around. The alleyways, though still beaten earth, had loose dust over their way. Their footprints only added to the scuffle, reminding Alik they were not the only ones who needed to pass with as few eyes to watch as they could wrangle.

The gloom thickened. Little even of the torchlight reached to alleys, but enough to see their way. At one corner, Constantine turned to survey the light rising over the walls.

"Waste of torches," he said.

"They'll just steal more," said Alik. "No pirate urges another not to waste, well, anything—it shows a want of faith in their skills—if they're really short of a thing they do a raid to go after it—and what if they all died tomorrow? Then it would really go to waste—and what's the point of a short life and a merry one if it's not merry?"

His voice echoed oddly from the walls about them. A light gleamed ahead—more evident from the shadows it cast than the light itself. Alik put a finger to his mouth. Constantine scowled, but as long as he was silent—

Alik crept closer. Maundering, nonsensical words, rambling tunelessly on, reached them. The growing light—grayish like dawn—made Constantine's set face all the clearer. The alleyway reached a barren room, marked only with dust. Gray light suffused it. On the beaten earth, an aged man, little more than skin and bones, sat and stared, maundering on.

Alik laid a hand on Constantine's arm and drew him around, behind the motionless man. The danger of his seeing them was little, but enough to be wary of, when it cost them nothing to avoid it. Constantine looked about as if seeking where the light came from, but he did not speak until they slid down the alleyway on the other side, and the walls hid them from the man.

There, his gaze shifted back. His voice was low. "Who was that?"

Alik kept his voice as low. "A captive wizard. Some, like Maximus, throw themselves into winning the pirates' favor with crafty spells. Some—" Like Hilarion, he thought. "—survive by trading little magics with slaves and pirates. And some—" His hand swept the air to take in the door. "—go mad."

"And some become wind-witches."

"Oh, no. That *honor* is reserved for those born here. Who had nowhere else to flee." Alik walked on. The gray light faded, leaving only torchlight.

At the next turn, Constantine's hand brushed his shoulder. His voice was softer than before. "Followed."

Alik saw nothing, but pointed to a corner. There, he gathered shadows about them both.

A youth appeared. Torchlight glittered on a knife in his hand, though from his dress he was a slave—Alik's gaze went to his face, and he stiffened. A nut-brown, square-faced youth, a little older and taller than him, and more solidly built.

Ivo.

Alik's gaze went back to the knife. Not just the blade glittered. The hilt had gleaming jewels, and Alik thought he recognized it. Pointing, he mouthed to Constantine—magic.

Constantine did not look concerned, and Alik felt no surprise.

Ivo continued toward them, unrelenting. His gaze was so steady that Alik realized that Ivo did not look at the corner, or even at them both, but at him. Constantine tensed beside him.

Alik dropped the shadows. "It's me. You don't need the knife."

Ivo started and did not move forward. "It's you I'm looking for. You could not witch yourself away." His voice dripped poison. "Who else would I look for? After the uproar you made? After I was your *student*?"

"I taught you a trick or two," said Alik. "In exchange for a few goods."

"You were my teacher," spat Ivo. He shifted as if to flank him. Alik turned to face the other youth. Constantine moved, but Alik could not turn his attention aside from Ivo.

"If I were your teacher," said Alik, "you would have to obey me." Only the knife's glitter kept him from laughter at the thought of Ivo's obeying anyone who could not force him.

Ivo laughed, shortly, muttered, and threw the torch into the air. It hung there, casting orange light and vast shadows, as Ivo turned back to Alik.

"After your treachery? After you fled the Red Hawk? Every wizardling in the port would cut off his hand for that chance! You can not even *bother* trying to win your noose."

Blame Hilarion, Alik thought, glancing at the knife for only a moment before looking back to Ivo's face. He was my teacher, I obeyed him, and he used his scrystone to show me, again and again, places that I could escape to.

He said, "You would think worse of that ship if you served on it."

Ivo's lip curled. "Heh. And *you* think you taught me all I know." He lunged.

His knife clattered against Constantine's sword.

Ivo looked up at the knight with no fear in his face. "So loyal," he whispered, "to *die* for him." He lifted his dagger toward his mouth, close enough that he could have kissed the pommel, and whispered, "Alik."

Constantine's left hand seized Alik and shoved him behind. His sword almost glowed from the light it caught as he pressed the attack, and steel clashed. Ivo scrambled back, and Constantine stopped, eying him warily, as if Ivo could flank him to get to Alik.

Alik grimaced. Wise, perhaps—he could not match Ivo with even ordinary blades.

Ivo's gaze met Constantine's and flickered away from those hellfire eyes. "You're a big one. What's your name?"

"Habrec," said Alik.

Ivo drew up the dagger toward his mouth again. Then he stopped and glared. Constantine's mouth twitched, and Ivo snarled and lunged again, with such furor that he almost made Constantine's greater reach and skill moot. Alik stepped back as blades furiously thrust and parried, and racked his mind for any wizardry that could aid. A light spell, even if he could cast one swiftly enough, would blind all three of them—as bad for flight as for fighting—and draw the pirates, eager for a hunt. They would laugh as loudly at the fool pirates who thought Alik had fled. . . .

Constantine's sword lashed out. Blood marred its edge and seeped from Ivo's arm.

Ivo snarled. "The two of you against the one of me." The gemstones glittered redly. Ivo looked thoughtful, his eyes narrowed.

Alik thought of a spell. As quick as he could, fighting to shift the air just so, he made a voice right by the hilt of Ivo's knife.

It whispered, "Ivo."

Ivo froze, staring at the knife as if Alik had transformed it into a snake. The hilt shifted in his hand, cutting, drawing blood. Ivo's mouth opened to scream.

Constantine's sword sliced through the air into Ivo's throat. Blood fountained, and the only cry to escape was a gurgle.

The blow had not cut Ivo's head off, but it landed at an improbable angle to the rest of his body, and even by torchlight Alik could see how the blood had darkened toward crimson. He stood very still and gulped as he tried to subdue his stomach. His empty stomach had no business heaving up, to burn his mouth, and he could not take his gaze from the widening pool of blood.

"Well done," said Constantine, going to clean his sword. "This time."

The knife glittered on the ground, despite the blood. Alik dropped to one knee to put his hand over it. The motion took his gaze from the body. He drew in quick sharp breaths and cast the shield spell, warding it from touch. Here he did not even have to worry about the knife pushing against it. Then he wrapped shadow about it, rendering it an undistinguishable lump.

Drawing a deep breath, he stood. He managed to keep his back to the body.

Constantine studied the dust. "We'd best be gone. No one heard us—" Obviously, Alik thought. "—but this is too traveled. Someone may notice, and try to curry favor."

Alik shook his head. "We'd best hide the body."

Constantine cocked an eyebrow, looking at the pool of blood.

Alik swallowed. He had done it before. He had even known the names of some slaves he had done it on. The one spell he had mastered by rote—the one spell that many a slave knew.

"You don't imagine—" His voice dripped scorn as he stood over the puddle. "—that pirates will let us be, when they trip over bodies or slip in the blood?"

He dropped to one knee again to incant the spell. The flesh was colder already, and the words sour and bitter in his mouth, but Ivo's blood flowed steadily, deep red, into the dust, which drank it up.

The ground still bore blood stains, but in the red dust, a man would have to look with care to see them, and nothing about this place would catch the eye for that. Alik stood. And bloodstains alone would not betray them, not in this port.

Constantine, impassive, swept the corpse to his shoulder. His gaze was steady on Alik. Alik reached up to snatch the torch from the air, and quenched its flames. Then, after a moment, he led Constantine back, not quite along the path they had taken. With the gray light reappearing, he pondered what room was best.

Then he heard the silence. After a frozen moment, he inched forward.

The wizard lay in a pool of his own blood. Alik stepped forward, staring. Who—why would even a pirate stab a harmless old madman? After having tolerantly let him live for so many years? Some even thought that harming him was bad luck.

Constantine eyed the wound. "The same blade. Or one much like it—but it looks like he tracked us through this place."

Alik swallowed, hard.

Constantine closed his eyes for a minute. Then he asked, "Do you want to hide this body, too?"

Alik shook his head. "Nothing to connect him to us." He wished his voice was not so thin.

Constantine nodded, contemplating the body again.

Praying? wondered Alik, and said, sharply, "We have to go. This was no tragedy to him."

"That's a tragedy in itself," said Constantine, almost gently.

"There." Alik jabbed his finger, pointing into one alley and a dark doorway there, to a musty room, laden with boxes and crates years ago and undisturbed since. Perhaps since before he had been born—or Ivo had been. Alik shuddered.

Constantine stirred up dust, until he laid the body behind some crates. As good a hiding place as any, and with the dust disturbed, he left no clear path to it. He paused a moment.

Alik scowled. "He hated me, because he *wanted* a chance to earn his noose."

Constantine straightened, his face muffled by the shadows. "He earned it. And more besides. You could have—"

"No, I could not," said Alik. "Many a witch-child has earned a noose even younger than I." If he had realized that early enough, he would have refused to learn the wind-witching. Or at least have tried to refuse. Hilarion might have insisted, for protection, since he had cared whether Alik lived or died.

He glared at Constantine.

Constantine glanced at the body again. "He said—but he is no witch-child—"

"What?" said Alik. "You don't believe that superstition, do you? A witch-child has to study like everyone else."

A bell's heavy note rang over them. Constantine looked sharply about. Alik's stomach curdled.

It rang again.

"A ship's returned," said Alik, sourly. Constantine would profit from the knowledge. "Come."

He picked his path. Soon, as the bell tolled yet again, they descended a side stair. Not to a particularly useful location for any other purpose, but gaps in the wall let them see the sea swells, touched by starlight and glancing torchlight, without so much as a flying fish rising above the waters.

The bell tolled, and the Tower of the Stone blazed with light. Blinking a moment let Alik see the light pouring from the height of it, in blue and white and green beams, making the waves glisten, flooding the port with light and shadow, even sketching out the last scraps of cloud.

He could not make out much of the tower. Hilarion had always told him that it worked like a scrystone, but Alik had never seen how Hilarion had ever gotten close enough to tell.

The light beams twisted in air. Out of the brilliance, a ship sailed. Under the green light, the sails looked black; under the blue, a ghastly dark purple; but the white showed them scarlet. The ship sailed toward the docks.

Alik's mouth twisted. Especially when no scrystone did anything like that, and if one could have, Hilarion would have fled long before he took Alik on as a student.

The pirates swarmed toward the docks, calling to their fellows, hearing their returning cries. The ship tied up, they turned to the loot. Slaves, dragged from the buildings to the dock, or dragged, battered and beaten, from below the ship's deck, were burdened with great chests—many of them—but some chests two or three pirates took up. Alik's breath hissed out. That could not be good, loot that pirates did not entrust to slaves' hands.

Pirates, and staggering slaves, started the torch-lit procession through the port, to flaunt the treasure. The torchlight flared over the walls as they vanished among the buildings, and cast enormous shadows, distorted images of loot-bearing figures, against the cliffs.

Alik let his breath out. The pirates would pile it in great heaps and rejoice over it, but that would also mean they swarmed over the port in their celebrations.

He glanced at Constantine. "We should go. Now." He did not have much hope, but they set out through the alleyways by yet another path—to hear the pirates' uproarious glee.

He still hoped, a little, but casting about soon showed that pirates, rejoicing, had indeed crossed every path in the port, cutting off every way to the Tower of Winds.

And their bragging revealed that the ship had taken cannons and shot. They would be well-armed for their next raid on a city—and the Witch Prince already made the plans for that.

When Alik turned to Constantine, all the play of light from the moving torches could not hide his set expression.

The words felt flat in Alik's mouth. "We can't get in. We have to wait for morning."

Constantine's expression hardened to steel. For a moment, Alik thought he would refuse with no heed to the revelers about, who would kill them both as part of their amusements.

His voice was curt and low. "Where can we sleep?"

"A storeroom. We can find something."

Constantine nodded. His mouth twisted. "We've done so already. Twice."

Alik led him off, this time more slowly. This close to the Tower of the Winds and their stone stronghold, the pirates thronged, whooping down this alleyway and that one. Once, as a procession of torches passed where Alik and Constantine crouched in shadow, Alik's eyes closed for a moment. If they just rested here, they would be closer, come morning.

Constantine poked him in the side.

Alik shifted his weight. The pirates had gone far enough away. He drew closer to the doorway, ready to dart over to the next slave alley.

A small boy, his eyes bruised with exhaustion, lugged a flagon far too large for him out of the alley. Alik's heart beat out the moments before they stole across, but they needed to move. The light from the stone illuminated their way, but it would not last forever, and then they would see no more than by torchlight.

In the next square, pirates argued. Not over loot, surprisingly this close to a return, but Alik did not linger to listen.

A dog barked, and Alik stopped. Slowly, he turned his head. Two pirates led out four dogs: great hunting hounds, one white as bone, one black as soot, one red as blood, and one green as grass growing on ruins where once a city had stood, before the pirates came. The dogs, tugging at their leashes, growled and snapped. Alik glanced at the pirates holding them. He did not recognize one, but the other was Fedor, who grinned, baring his teeth.

"Let Habrec muck about with cannon all he likes," Fedor bellowed. "He lets spies run about our stronghold—"

"They fled," shouted one pirate. With a mug of ale in hand, he slouched against the wall, and he sounded resentful of being roused.

"If that bratling could flee," said Fedor with a sneer, "he would have fled years ago and taken Hilarion with him. He knows a jester's tricks with light and color, and Habrec was a fool not to see that was the spell before the—throne."

Some pirates muttered about the stone, but Fedor looked at his hounds.

"These beauties will hunt them down and show him. They must have turned invisible."

Alik wondered whether Fedor had found anything to give them the scent. Biting his lip, ignoring a sideways glance from Constantine, he lifted his hands for the spell and sent a breeze across the way, wafting his own scent before the beasts.

The blood-red hound bayed, deep in its chest. Alik worried his lip. If it lost the scent, the hound would cast about, searching—he sent the breeze off, toward the doorway. The other hounds bayed, and joined in the chase.

Alik started off along the way. Someone might hear the footsteps, a slave might come along, but the hounds were more dangerous than either circumstance. He glanced into the room at every chink, and sent the breeze on.

Constantine shadowed him, silently. He could only hope that the knight had guessed at his spellcraft; he could not add a voice to the noise they already made.

"There, that does it," said Fedor, full of malice.

Alik drew a deep breath and sent the breeze down a roundabout route. He scampered for the room it would eventually lead to. He had won himself a moment, with the shorter path, but he wrestled with ways to get the hounds off their track. Spices, he thought. Conjured rightly, they would work as well on the hounds as the jester's lights had on the throne room. But for it, he needed to find spices, and fresh ones as well.

He reached the room, and found it filled with pirates swilling fine wines—the ship must have borne more than weapons—and jeering at Fedor's folly.

Alik's eyes narrowed. For a moment, he thought of Habrec, but in this uproar, the throne room would be worse than the Tower of Winds. He had to act quickly. He stopped, his breath so harsh he half-thought the pirates would hear it, but they did not turn. In the middle of this crew stood Captain Ogier, his mouth twisted by the livid scar across his cheek—the scar that new slaves were warned marked out his cruelty, even among pirates.

The hounds' baying grew louder, as they raced about the loop and closer once again.

"Fedor's little toys." Ogier swilled more wine. A scrawny girl, dead eyed, came over with the flagon of wine. The hounds bayed again, Ogier jerked the tankard, and the wine slopped. The girl's eyes widened—perhaps the first feeling she had shown in months—and Ogier backhanded her, sending wine over the floor like blood and throwing her into the wall.

The pirates roared with mirth. Ogier grinned. Then he shivered. Alik's mouth twisted into a smile; he increased the breeze, letting it play over Ogier.

The hounds, baying, burst into the room, their eyes brilliantly avid, their mouths lolling open, their legs moving with grace and speed, until the blood-red one, in the lead, leapt on Ogier. Blood splattered, invisible on it, but vivid on the other three as they pounced, maws biting and splattering themselves with more scarlet.

Shouts of outrage rose. Some scrambled to haul the dogs off Ogier. Others, more prudently, drew blades to stab the beasts, or went to club them. Fedor stared from the doorway as if wondering what Ogier had done, when a pirate struck him with a meaty fist, and Fedor's followers surged into the fight.

Alik, his breath steadying, half-wished to stay and see if Ogier died, if Fedor was killed, but he turned his face away. Constantine showed no more approval than a stone. They picked their way out, along corridors, and the sound of fighting followed. Once or twice, Alik glimpsed a pirate stabbing another, neither man having been among the crowd where the fight started, but he had seen too many brawls to hope it did much damage. More than once, he hid them in shadows from slaves, who scurried by faster than usual, their eyes enormous. Alik wondered if they would see anyone in their fright. He looked at the floor as footsteps scurried off. He supposed a city looked worse like after a raid.

"This way," he said, thinly. Constantine, mute, his expression impervious, followed. Alik tried not to think on how—even not counting the dead from the brawl—he had already killed more men than Habrec and Constantine had wanted him to. His jaw set. At least, more than they had wanted him to, then. Who knows how many would have died at his hand by now if he had returned to Habrec's service?

Another musty, out-of-the-way room—Alik wondered, as he never had before, how much of their plunder the pirates tossed aside. He dropped to the floor, not caring much. The light from the stone was fading; it was well that they wanted only to sleep.

"Here." Constantine thrust something before him. His nose recognized it: bread and dried meat. Constantine held an open bag, the same bag they had eaten from during the day.

Constantine snorted and sat himself. "Your pirates aren't the only ones with wizardry. Now, eat."

Slowly, Alik's hands went up to take it. When he bit off a mouthful of bread, it was rough on his tongue, and he felt ravenous. He bolted both so swiftly that he barely tasted either.

Constantine, not half done with his meal, snorted and handed him a water bottle. It held sweeter water than that from barrels. Alik drank and drank.

"Your pirate king is not popular among the pirates," said Constantine. The light from the stone, fading but not gone, played over his face and cast white bars and dark shadows across it. He took another bite of bread.

Alik snorted and felt water slip from his mouth onto his face. He lowered the bottle.

Constantine went on. "So why do they not gut him and get themselves another? A short life and a merry one—they'd be merrier without him."

"The stone." Alik held out the bottle, and Constantine took it back. "The World's Ways. Where would they be without his mastery of it?" He smiled, spreading his hand.

But the World's Ways could not be hard to master. Habrec had done it, when he knew no other magic. To be sure, nonetheless, the pirates had grumbled but never even tried to overthrow him. He rubbed his eyes. He needed rest.

"Get some sleep, Alik. Unless you do not wish to be up with the dawn."

Alik forced his breath out. For all that he had seen and endured growing up, he would not sleep, not so soon after those hounds nearly hunted them down. And the pirates' revelries, or fights, still sounded in the night, louder than most nights. More men would die there. His mouth tightened. He could hope they were all men who had earned their noose—which, he had to concede, Constantine had not. He glanced at the knight, whose face he could not read. Hilarion would approve of his having saved his life, he thought. He sighed as softly as he could. How could he sleep when such thoughts turned in his head?

Still, he lay on the earth, using his arm for a pillow, and closed his eyes. He could rest if he could not sleep.

He felt Constantine's hand on his shoulder—a moment later, it seemed, but gray morning light seeped into the room and made it look still dingier. Even the ruddy shade of the dust could not brighten it, and the still air was bitterly cold.

He staggered to his feet, stretching his arms against the stiffness. Constantine handed him more bread, this time with dried fruit. Alik ate, not quite so fiercely, but quickly. Morning meant slaves moving about, eager to do what they could before the pirates roused. Earlier might have been better, but there would have been slaves, even then.

He brushed off the crumbs and led the way through the dawn.

The pirates had settled down to drinking, eventually. Many sprawled across the streets, often with mug still in hand.

"They must get drenched when it rains," said Constantine, his voice low.

Alik glanced up. The sky still held clouds, if not the blanket of the day before. Hilarion, on days like this, would marvel about those clouds.

"It never rains. Not here. That is why nothing green grows." He walked on, swiftly, picking their way far more directly than he had dared by night.

Even the corpses did not make him flinch. Though the thought ran around his head that there must have been more. These dead could only be those that died so late that the pirates had not cared about tripping over them. After the brawl over the hounds, they would have bellowed for the slaves to haul the dead away.

Some of these might even have died from cracking their heads, falling over while dead drunk. His hand formed a fist. They could not all have died in the brawl he set off.

Constantine glanced sideways at him after another pool of blood.

"I wonder how many will hang for killing," said Alik.

Constantine raised an eyebrow.

"Part of the law. Brawling's all right, but you've got to duel in order to kill—at least, to kill pirates. And—" He shrugged. "They've all earned their nooses."

Constantine grunted. "Unless they claim that all who fought the dead men also died."

"Likely," Alik admitted. In an empty street, he glanced at the Tower of Winds. It loomed, but the spells on it were nothing like those on the Tower of the Stone.

It even had slave stairs, which was its greatest weakness.

Constantine looked about at the dingy buildings in the gray light. Alik chanted the unlocking spells. Long ago, a wizard had sagely feared what would happen if he did not arrive swiftly enough, and slaves had passed the knowledge on, year by year, without—Alik opened the door and gestured to Constantine, who followed him in—without Habrec even wondering why he could bellow for wine and have it in moments.

Or so he had heard. He closed the door and let his eyes adjust. The light was less here than anywhere else but the corridors at night. Alik looked up the stairway. Narrow and plain, of course. Such dust as there was lay, ruddy, in odd corners. Being Hilarion's student might have kept him from servant duties and from being stabbed by some drunken oaf, but it had also kept him from here.

They didn't have time for him to let Constantine know of his ignorance. He strode to the stairs and climbed. Light mounted, steadily, almost with each stair, until they reached the first platform. The tower still went up, but Habrec's chambers were here, where he did not have to continue to climb. Alik put his hand to the door. Not like the Tower of Stone where secrecy was that much more valued.

The door opened easily, to a back corridor, but already he could see astrolabes, maps, sextants, compasses, and other things that Hilarion's teaching had not included.

None of which mattered. Alik strode in and looked about. Habrec had had it furnished with cabinets and desks and chairs, all of fine wood, polished to a mirror's surface; even if none of it matched, none had been damaged by its capture. Papers lay everywhere. And piles of books—Hilarion had taught him using every book he could lay his hands on and had not gotten a third of one of those piles.

They couldn't all be about navigation, Alik thought.

Constantine appraised the room. "How does Habrec give orders to his captains?"

Alik blinked, casting back his memory. He had never come this close, and Hilarion had never dared scry too closely, but he had seen them set out. "Boxes. Wooden boxes, metal bound."

Constantine nodded, looking satisfied. "Thought these looked familiar." He walked over to the stacked boxes in one corner, and Alik felt a fool.

"There's the free life for you—getting your orders in a box just like you were a captain in the navy." Constantine snorted. "Down to the same boxes."

He sounded as if he knew it all before this, thought Alik, bitterly. He looked over and was glad he had not said that aloud. The box still bore the royal crest, even if the metal had dulled with time.

"Dare say that he thinks the rings necessary—" Constantine put his hand to the crest. Alik could not quite follow what he did, but the box slid open, soundlessly. Constantine let out his breath, and Alik edged over to see the paper inside. Constantine took it out and straightened it to read the orders to attack Kingsport.

Alik listened for a minute, but Constantine added nothing more, and he did not suddenly realize that he had misheard him.

"So that's it, then," said Alik.

Constantine nodded, and scowled at the smudges of red dust on the letter and inside the box.

"Oh, put it back," said Alik, "but don't close it."

Constantine eyed him but obeyed. Alik raised his hand and incanted. A whisper of air slid over the letter, picking up dust. Constantine slid shut the box, and the air whispered over it as well. Alik slowly backed toward the slave stairs, letting the breeze catch every fleck of dust. Constantine, warily, eying the dust, edged past him.

Alik closed the door with the dust on his side. Then he swept it to one corner, to hide among the shadows and the other dust. The slaves might not betray them, but best to not give them the chance.

He let his breath out and listened. Outside, nothing more stirred than had before their venture. A grin plastered itself to his face, and Alik forced himself to remember they had to both get away uncaught and get the word out. Their knowledge did the king, and Kingsport, no good. Habrec perhaps had never learned of the stairs, because no slave had ventured to futilely steal from him by the stairs, when there was nowhere to flee with the gains. Even they had work ahead of them.

But Constantine knew that they had only gained the knowledge because of him.

Quiet as mice—down the stairs, out the door, through the alleyways—they went. Slaves hurried about, and even some pirates moved, stirring and moaning, and cursing the drink and the fool slave who had needed a good thrashing.

Already the bodies were gone, and the blood conjured into the dust to make it all the more red.

That thought took the edge of his elation, but no more than the edge. They stole onward, through hovels even more decrepit than those they had used the day before, and out, onto the rocky shore, where jagged rocks hid them from the docks. Alik drew in a deep breath of the salt air, blowing inland, smelling of nothing but the sea. The sky turned from gray to shades of eggshell white and yellow as day approached.

"Here?" said Constantine.

Alik nodded. Constantine surveyed the stones and walked over to the narrowest place leading to the shore. There he drew his sword.

"You won't be able to buy me time enough, if they find us," said Alik.

"That would depend on how far you had gotten in the spell by that time," said Constantine, coldly.

Alik looked away. He felt the heat in his face, and he knew the red would be brilliant. Keeping his back to Constantine, he began the spell. Hilarion had not known it, and the royal wizard had all but taught him by rote. And to get even a single word over land and sea to echo in a far distant room—he concentrated.

When the final words of the incantation slipped from his mouth, there was an expectant pause, the air seeming to stand still about him.

Alik said, "Kingsport," and the air seemed to shudder and, after a moment, let the breeze in again. The spell had finished.

He looked about. Without his noticing, the colors of dawn had given way to plain daylight. He grinned. It had, after all, been little more difficult than hiding that dagger, he thought merrily. Constantine looked up. Feeling light-headed, Alik pondered what to do next. If they sneaked onto the attacking fleet, they could escape the port entirely.

Constantine put up his sword before leading the way back among the buildings. The walls cut off the sea breeze, leaving them trapped in dusty air, though the daylight still brightly lit the way. Alik trailed after, knowing they had no need for haste. They walked on, as the sun slowly rose to shine through the thin clouds over the alleys, and Alik noted that Constantine had mastered the path.

The towers grew clearer ahead of them, they drew nearer to where people lived, and the morning roused yet more. Alik pondered the next days. Looking for a way to escape. No doubt the king had better things for his knights to do than linger in a pirate port after discovering what they had come for.

Unless. He blinked, remembering. He wondered how long Domenic had stayed here, with no chance of escape. If the king tried to press him into staying as a spy forever. . . .

His mouth set. If the royal forces did enough damage to the pirates, they would be able to leave freely.

Then he remembered the hawks.

His mouth twisted. Even Constantine would have to concede that if they could, they should flee rather than die uselessly under Maximus's spell, but the hawks were a greater danger than Constantine, or the king's orders. It did make escape rather urgent.

But they were near enough to the center of the stronghold that he did not dare just speak to him. He crept closer, but Constantine still walked briskly, and there was no time to draw him aside.

Shouts and whoops rose ahead of them, raucous—cruel. Alik grimaced, wondering who had fallen afoul of the pirates. When Constantine scowled and walked toward the noise, Alik followed. Slaves scurrying away sent them into corners behind the shadows, but then Constantine walked on, and Alik wondered when to broach the matter. They were unlikely to have a better chance. If the uproar spread far enough, if it distracted the pirates enough to let them steal a boat, they might escape.

Perhaps even with Domenic.

The bellow came from a square before. Constantine stopped in the slave alley. Alik caught up and froze. Constantine looked so horrified that Alik was afraid to look. He muttered the shadow spell about them and still did not turn.

The pirates' shouts rose, and slowly, as if dragged by a thread of curiosity, Alik turned toward the gap to peer out.

Boden stood there, towering over those about. Boden, Habrec's witless right hand, violent, enchanted, enormous. And before him, sword in hand, Domenic stood, looking ready to fight to the death and full aware that the death would be his.

Alik felt sick to his stomach. Boden did not run free, not here, not in the pirates' stronghold. Stupidly loyal, he did only what Habrec told him to do.

Boden's heavy club came down, knocking Domenic flat.

"Ho! What happens?" Habrec strode in, scowling.

"No kill!" said Boden, pointing.

Habrec snorted. "So *some* pirates can obey their laws." He stood over Domenic, who shifted a little and then lay still. Alik, swallowing, realized that the knight could not rise.

Habrec's voice lowered. "I, however, am King of the Pirates. I can kill. It is my duty to kill, in chains, those who break the pirates' laws."

A murmur went about the pirates—none too loudly, as no man wanted to offend the master of the Ways of the World.

Habrec crouched by Domenic. "And since I have detected a whisper spell coming from these parts, I have set a spell to ensure that no such spell goes out again. And—I have changed my mind!"

He stood then, looking about the assembled pirates. "Ready yourself, men! We go to lay waste the city of Fairington!"

Pirates roared approval. Alik felt the blood seeping from his face. Slowly, feeling he moved like an ancient man, he turned to face Constantine.

Constantine could look even more horrified than when he saw Domenic's plight. Alik swallowed.

Pirates surged forward to haul Domenic up. Domenic did not scream, and if he groaned, the uproar overwhelmed the sound, but his face contorted.

Alik and Constantine scuttled away like mice, but mice would never have had his spell ready to hide them in shadows—forever, thought Alik. Futilely, because those hawks would hunt them out soon enough.

He did not know why, but he scuttled about the alleyways until they could look over the sea. The chains hung there, not empty, even now. A woman's body slumped against the stone. The dancer, Alik realized, and wondered how she had offended, or even if she had.

Futile, he thought, turning his face away. Madness. Though they lurked in shadow, he should never have come here and risked the danger. Even with the hawks lurking, waiting only for the moment that Maximus realized how Alik had stopped them.

But he did not pull back.

Pirates hauled Domenic out. He had more bloodstains and bruises than when they had carried him off, they had stripped off his brightly colored clothing, and they reached for the chains. One taunt reached over the waters: they had even brought him female companionship.

Constantine's hand touched his shoulder. Constantine nodded along the alleyway, and Alik mutely followed.

"He won't last long in that condition," said Constantine, grimly.

"Habrec will have a wizard heal him," said Alik. "It's the only time a slave can get healed." The time that Habrec had besieged a city, only to lift it in return for a chest of medicines—it had been for pirates. He had understood little of the attack and the demand, but he remembered the long hours of his mother's babbling in fever and finally going still.

When they stopped in a dust-laden alleyway, the heat was mounting. Alik dropped to the ground, sitting with his legs bent under him and his head bowed. The hotter it was, the sooner Domenic would die. If Habrec had always known who Domenic was, they had been played for fools. If meeting with them had revealed him—Alik's mouth tightened in a spasm—he had killed yet another man. More than Habrec had demanded of him. . . .

Constantine came up beside him, with water.

Alik drank.

Constantine said, "It's only one knight you've saved."

"Saved?" snapped Alik. "Have you forgotten the hawks and my spell on them? I haven't *saved* you. It will not last because—"

It felt as if someone had opened a window in a dark room—a sudden illumination, so brilliant that he forgot Constantine entirely and stared into air.

Then he closed his mouth and stood. His legs felt stiff already, but he said, "I know what we must do."

"Go outside your Witch-Prince's spell to cast another whisper spell?" Constantine's voice was dry.

"Maximus would have his hawks on us before we crossed half the distance. No, we must do—something else."

Explaining that the spells Maximus used could be twisted would take too long, even if the knight believed him. He had not even explained how Maximus enchanted the tower with the World's Ways in it, to keep people out, and this would take even longer. He looked up at Constantine and set his jaw.

Constantine glared at him. "Is that something else stand here until we rot?"

Alik shrugged and turned aside, calculating. Sunlight shone down the alleyway. No longer gray with dawn, but it would be hours before it turned orange with evening. They would sit about for hours somewhere, and it would be best for that place to be as close as he could get it. Arriving late would ruin all.

"We have to go." But he stood a moment longer, his eyes closed, as he traced out in his mind the route to Maximus's chambers—the best route, not the fastest. The thing they needed least was prying eyes, and they did not, yet, lack time.

He opened his eyes again. Constantine looked angry enough to strike him.

"To save Domenic, no doubt." Acid dripped from his voice.

"Men," said Alik, "have died in the chains in less time than this will take—but maybe."

Despite the rising heat, he set out briskly. His stomach roiled. Actually putting his plan into words would make its absurdity all too plain.

He remembered the hawks. The two of them would be lucky if the hawks only tore them apart—if the hawks caught them. He walked on.

And on. At times, he wondered whether he had taken a too safe route, especially when Constantine had them stop to eat. They had hours, but stealing about the stronghold could take hours.

Then a slave hurried down the corridor, and his heart
hammering, he hid himself and Constantine in shadows. More
and more as they drew nearer.

But even hiding from slaves, they eased down the alleyways
away from the pirates. As they reached their object, shadows
slanted over the alleyways, but the sky was still blue, and the
sunlight golden, laden with dust motes—not even orange—with
afternoon.

"Maximus's chambers," said Alik, his voice low. "He will
emerge soon—"

Constantine snorted. "And you want him to set no hawks on
us."

"Among other things," said Alik. "First that—"

He froze, but it was too late. Fool, fool, fool, he had let his
plan fill his thoughts, had trusted in how little the slaves came
here, and now a girl-slave studied them in the shadows of alley.
She—of course—held the tray that would slide into Maximus's
room without disturbing him until he wished to eat, and Alik felt
the bitter taste of his failure.

She glided forward, not taking her gaze from them. Younger
even than he was, and a bruise lay across her face, marked by a
heavy hand.

When she came even with them, she met Alik's gaze for a
moment and turned her gaze back to the alleyway.

She was out of sight when Alik managed to whisper, "This
way." His heart beat—not faster, but harder. He had been saved
from his own folly once. He could not even think of risking such
danger again. They slid down the last of the alleys with feet as
soft as shadows'.

He had known the shield had not failed—the hawks would
have descended in moments—but seeing a hopeless jumble of
metallic feathers still calmed his heart. They did not rise up so
high that he could not, once he got close, see how they trailed
back to the bowl. Alik let out a sigh of relief. Only one thing to

deal with, then. Maximus, absorbed in his studies, would not have time to restore this spell before he restored the other.

"There," he said, pointing to beside the door. "You will stand there, and I will shadow you. It will not last once you strike, so you must make your blow count."

Constantine studied him for a silent minute. "And you?"

"I will not shadow myself. It will have to be you who strikes."

"What fool plan are you working?"

"One that will not work if you are not shadowed and ready to strike," said Alik. He surprised himself, with how tart he could make the words. "Or if he hears voices here, to warn him."

Constantine scowled but obeyed, and Alik shadowed him. He stepped back, breathing a sigh of relief. He could have explained on the way, but he had this dread that if he did, Constantine would see what a foolish plan it was, and forbid it. At least with the jester's tricks, he had known the spells. This turned on the hope that he could master Maximus's spells quickly.

It was a foolish plan, and Constantine might well reject it. Even without a wiser one.

Alik turned. Constantine could not see the sky from the shadows of the arched doorway. Even if he could, he would not know what to look for. Unless he remembered, from the earlier day, Alik had said that Maximus needed to cast a spell with the new moon.

Alik walked about, looking, until he found a gap in the buildings that let him watch both the western sky and the doorway. He glanced back and forth, moving little more than Constantine did, as the sunlight grew orange, and then the sky took on color in bands: rose, orange, yellow, all of them in hazy shades. And then, just above them in the hazy blue, a narrow scrap of moon, colored golden in the sunset.

A bell chimed within, and Alik winced. Of course. Maximus leave his books long enough to see whether the new crescent moon had risen? Of course he had set a spell to keep watch for him.

He turned from the sunset. He scarcely dared to breathe. If this went awry, they, and Domenic, and all at Fairington, would die.

His breath eased out. Except for the unlucky at Fairington. So it must not go awry.

A shadowy figure shuffled out, as if too stiff from sitting to move freely. Alik thought he heard mumbling, but not enough to be sure of it, even when straining to hear. Light sifted in on the figure, revealing that his hair was dark gray and his robes parchment white, and that he held something in his hand. Alik bit his lip.

A startled cry announced that he had seen the bowl, and the birds. Alik drew a deep breath, stepped forward, and threw another shield spell, to encircle Maximus.

For long minutes, Maximus only poked at the birds, paying neither Alik nor his shield any heed. Alik waited, his hands forming fists that he released as soon as he noticed, his heart hammering out the moments, until, finally, Maximus looked up. His gaze reached Alik, and he stood, blinking like a day-blinded owlet.

Then he drew a sharp breath. "Hilarion's brat!"

Alik bowed.

"Making trouble—what does Hilarion want, this time?"

Alik blinked. He had not dreamed that Maximus's studies could keep him from knowing that Hilarion was dead, and he wondered what Hilarion had done last time, but—

"What a fool you are!" It surprised Alik, how he could make his voice ring. "You can't take your nose from your books long enough to learn that I sailed as a wind-witch—and on so shoddy a ship that I came back to defy the Witch-Prince to his face!"

"Witch-Prince?" Maximus's lip curled. "The fool has half a spell, and that one's useless without that great gaudy stone of his!"

Two, at least, though Alik, and then forced his attention back.

"Impudent brats who think him a wizard are—" He raised a hand. Alik braced himself, and Maximus's mouth shifted into something like a smile. "No threat at all."

Flame gushed from his hand, burst against the shield, and flooded back. A moment, Maximus stood, looking bewildered and even a little singed.

He broke the spell before it harmed him much, Alik reminded himself. He could not expect Maximus to destroy himself so easily.

"As opposed," Alik said, "to a wizard who has to cast his spell by the light of the new moon—to use its waxing to fortify his meager spellcraft!"

"As opposed—" Maximus put his hands out, and his words cut off. Alik fought to keep his face mask-like, as if he did not know the nature of the spell he had cast.

But Maximus hesitated too long. Every moment gave the wizard time to think, and so a chance to realize.

"As opposed," said Alik, "to a wizard who let a mere boy trap him! It's not just this way—I have encircled you, held you entirely—"

Maximus cackled. Alik felt his face contort and was shocked by the horror and fear he actually felt. If things went wrong here—

"Such a foolish pup!" Maximus pushed out with his hands, ready to show Alik that any shield of his could easily be broken out of, from within, by main force.

Alik's heart beat out the moments.

Maximus burst through the shield and staggered into the corridor. Constantine's sword swept through the air. Maximus's throat, completely unguarded, parted before its edge, and blood fountained, brilliantly red even in the gloom.

Maximus's face showed not even surprise as his head tumbled over the earth, spewing a trail of blood.

His stomach roiling, Alik dived to snatch what had been in Maximus's hands, trying to snag it before blood sloshed over it in its fall. He failed and stood there with it dripping gore.

"The water," said Alik.

Constantine raised an eyebrow as he pulled out the bottle, but he sloshed the water over it. Not all the blood washed off, but enough for him to see a ring of silver, set with green and blue jewels, too large even for Constantine's arm—how suitable. Alik drew a deep breath without looking at the body.

"I need other things, from in there."

Constantine nodded, but his gaze was on the body. "You lured him out with remarkable ease."

Alik laughed—and choked it off, frightening at the wild note he heard. He fought for a moment to steady his voice before he spoke. "Hilarion always said that his reclusiveness would kill him. And so it did. He didn't even know you existed."

He strode off. With the death, they had no choice but swiftness.

The rooms themselves were lit with gray light. Alik flinched. He forced himself to glance about the clutter on tables and cabinets—and flinched again, remembering not the dead madman, but Hilarion. The scrystone glittered there, and more stones, with minor virtues, nothing that Maximus would prize— and Alik forced his gaze away, searching while his thoughts would not leave the question of how long Maximus had waited after Hilarion's death to seize them.

Then, Maximus had not realized he was dead.

Alik's mouth twitched as he glanced over books. They had hustled him off to be a wind-witch quickly enough. They could have done the same to all that Hilarion had kept, and Maximus had taken what he would not prize, without realizing its source.

None of them would help him escape, or he and Hilarion would have long ago left the port. He knew what he wanted, and still looked about.

Once he saw it, the glinting mirror was unmistakable. Alik snatched it and fled to the doorway.

"Maximus didn't need that," Constantine said. "Whatever you intend to do to his spell."

"Maximus," said Alik, "was just going to renew the spell." He walked past the knight. He needed the new moon's light even more than Maximus would have. Some back routes would have kept them from sight, but he set out by the straightest route. He barely looked to see whether pirates could see them as they fled between alleyways; they needed the speed too much.

Constantine sometimes glanced at the crossways, but he did not argue.

Alik felt, with every step, as if a dagger pricked his back. But they reached the Tower of the Stone. The dirt here was hardly packed; it still astounded Alik that he had spied here with the scrystone, or that Hilarion had allowed it. The spells on the tower would not let him in the flesh.

But he had. And Maximus had cast the spells that kept the World's Ways safe here.

He set the mirror on the earth. It could be used to reveal as well as to reverse. And here he needed both—to run Maximus's spell backwards from the mirror, and to reveal the spell that had to be reversed. He drew a deep breath. He had cast both before.

"You might be able to stop the pirates long enough for me to finish the spell," he said, managing to keep his voice steady. "It depends on when they interrupt us."

A ghost of a smile appeared on Constantine's mouth, for only a moment, but he turned to stand watch.

Alik let his breath out. A reversal would not only need his knowledge of the spell, but knowledge of how it worked; he could not do it by rote. Kneeling, he began to sketch out the circle, from the hours when Hilarion had let him test the scrystone, to watch so closely he could know the spell. A protection spell! When he had never quite believed Hilarion that the World's Ways acted like a scrystone.

He plopped the ring in the circle, and put the mirror to reflect it properly. At least, there was no better place to unravel the spell.

Or die.

He finished the circle and stood. For a moment, he contemplated the tower and the walls; then he looked back at the circle. It seemed like threads of light, white and blue and green, extended from the ring to—

Alik stared at it for a minute. Then his mouth curved. No, the thread extended *to* the ring, from the stone. He looked up to see the woven threads through the tower. Maximus had used the stone to twist the very path to the stone. Alik's smile deepened. He did not even need to reverse it, with the threads.

Constantine shifted, but Alik could not turn his attention to see it. He need to see—

A sharp noise, of shattering, had him blink and glance sideways. The mirror lay in a thousand glittering shards, with a rock in their midst. Alik whirled around. Constantine, sword in hand, braced against three pirates, approaching but not in sword's reach.

One was Habrec.

The pirates had not discovered them by chance.

Alik bit his lip but was already reaching for the ring. He had to tuck it under his arm to cast a spell—simple and swift, something used to entertain any crowd. With it in hand, he called, "Constantine! Look at me!"

Constantine whirled around. The pirates lunged, and Alik hurled the spell. Light burst behind Constantine's back. Alik, looking away, caught only glimpses of brilliance, not enough to blind, though plenty enough to make him blink.

That would be seen by every slave and every pirate not already sunk in drunken slumber. And it would hold these three off only for moments.

Constantine ran toward him. Alik, still blinking, scuttled into the tower, hearing Constantine come after, but not daring to take his gaze from a ribbon of white. An explosion of curses from outside told him they had escaped, but Constantine's footsteps slowed behind them.

Alik turned. Constantine looked about the hallway—or, at any rate, turned his face this way and that. Alik was not sure whether he saw anything. He looked down to where blue and white twisted together, reached out to grab Constantine's hand, and despite his flinch, put the hand to the ring.

Constantine blinked, looking about.

"We follow the threads—Maximus must have used the World's Ways to conceal the way in—"

"Does Habrec have one of these?"

Alik flinched. "He would have to."

They went on, not so quickly as they had before, with the ring held awkwardly between them. Still, thought Alik stoutly, this was better than reversing the spell. Only Habrec could follow them now.

Which made him cock his ears for any step.

The thread went on and on, without twisting, or rising. Alik bit his lip. The stone was at the height of the tower, and he could not see how they could reach it without rising, but he also thought they had traveled farther than the tower was wide.

Then, ahead of them, a glow held a thousand such strands, on their own level. And a growl of rage came from behind them.

Constantine whirled, sword in hand, and parried Habrec's blow.

"No!" shouted Alik and threw up his hand, moving through the gestures he had seen Maximus perform. A tangle of lights sprang up between them, and Alik hurled it into Habrec's face.

Constantine must have seen something; he stepped back. Habrec's scream of fury was muffled with distance, though Alik could still see him.

Constantine turned and strode off. Alik, supposing the World's Ways was bright enough for him to see, scrambled after, still holding the ring. Constantine certainly did not hesitate, though once in the doorway, he stopped. Alik scooted around him.

The World's Ways glowed before them. Large enough to fill Alik's cupped hands—larger than the scrystone—rounded smooth, with white and green and blue shifting through its depths every now and again showing little images of far-off things, like the scrystone.

Alik grinned. He should have trusted Hilarion. He tucked the ring under his arm and reached out to take the stone. This might actually work.

A snarl of fury sounded from the doorway. For a moment. Alik stood frozen, wondering how Habrec could have reached here so quickly. Constantine's sword swung to face him; Constantine had never put it up, or even cleaned it, after the last meeting. Alik drew a deep breath and closed his eyes to concentrate on the stone. Swords clashed, and he flinched, and forced his thoughts back to the stone. It could not be too difficult, when Habrec had mastered it. He knew where he wanted, more than he ever had with the scrystone, but finding it and nowhere else was more urgent—

When he opened his eyes again, the tangled ribbons of light showed, not a pirate ship, but Domenic hanging in his chains.

He did not even look up at the lights, but shouts came; pirates were watching their prisoner.

Then, he had known his first light spell would rouse them.

"Constantine!" he shouted. Habrec flinched, throwing up his arm to shield his eyes, and Constantine broke off and ran toward him. Moments later, Habrec snarled and ran after. Alik wished he had a light spell, but—no matter. He jumped through. Constantine leapt after him, and Habrec after him. Constantine turned with a snarl as fierce as Habrec's and rejoined the fight, standing braced before Dominic without yielding an inch.

Alik shoved both stone and ring into a niche in the wall and ran. They did not keep the keys far off.

He stepped through the doorway into the building. The key ring hung the wall, he could see it, but a pirate stood between him and it, and though his hand was steady, he was reaching for his sword. Alik yanked his knife and stabbed. The pirate's shout would draw more, but the spewing blood gave him a moment to fly by and snatch the keys, as the pirate's hand leapt to staunch the wound.

"You cursed—"

Alik stabbed again. The pirate parried the blow. Not easily—but he was not drunk enough to be easy prey. Alik lunged, and the knife struck into his throat. The knife drove too deeply for Alik to pull out, but the gurgle in the pirate's throat said he had stopped him well enough.

At the price of not being able to stop another—Alik ran. No time to think, even—especially—when he heard the pirate thud to the floor.

Habrec and Constantine fought furiously, blocking the walkway. Alik snagged the World's Ways and, his back firmly against the wall, away from the fall to the waters, bent his attention on it again. Easy this time to see what he wanted—he leapt through a tangle to drop beside Domenic and kneel to unlock the chains.

With the key clicking in the lock, Domenic stirred a little and watched Alik with unreadable eyes. The chains fell free, and Domenic tried to push off the ground, steadying himself on Alik's arm.

Swords flashing in their hands, pirates stormed out the doorway behind Habrec where—Alik pushed Domenic's hand to the wall and seized the World's Ways. As if he could save them. He had thought he had realized that he might not, but failure was sour in his mouth. Habrec would just jump through any tangle he made. Any attempt to distract him would take out Constantine as well. He no longer had his knife. Even if he could find Domenic a sword, and Domenic could fight, they would have only two against—

For a moment, Alik could not breathe. Then he closed his eyes and concentrated again. He heard Domenic move and opened his own eyes. A smooth, mirror-like floor spread through the tangle. He leapt without looking for more, went sprawling, and scrambled away on hands and knees without daring to rise, or even to look up from the pale marble; it would take too much time. He did not know how he held onto the World's Ways, but he heard Domenic follow.

Moments later, Constantine sprang after. Habrec and the pirates roared, and surged through.

Inside the hall, glittering with mirrors and candles, scores of swords sprang up, encircling Constantine and the pirates, engulfing Domenic and Alik. Constantine, facing Habrec, was firmly drawn back by the royal guard. Habrec and the pirates turned back.

Ready to laugh, Alik clutched the World's Ways and dismissed the tangle, leaving him clutching an uncommon-looking stone that showed no signs of magic and fighting down laughter. Not that many looked at him, with the pirates standing before the guard, and the courtiers who, by law, had wear swords at court.

He looked from the slaughter. He himself had killed this hour. He had killed, to tell the truth, more before it. After the way this started—

The air did not smell of salt and sea. Something of dust, but that was what he himself had brought. The smell of blood joined that of burning candle wax. He studied the floor even as the clash of steel and other battle sounds ended, until men spoke of being rid of the bodies.

A grizzled knight spoke to Constantine and Domenic.

Domenic said, "I can stand long enough for a royal audience."

He sounded dazed, as if Alik knew any place other than the royal palace where he could bring swords to bear. Alik smiled a little. He had. . . he had. . . he looked into the depths of the World's Ways, and his smile faded as the thought of all that happened bore down on him.

"And you, Alik?" Constantine looked down at him.

Alik blinked.

"Can you stand long enough for a royal audience?"

A royal audience? Alik pondered a moment. This one, he guessed—he hoped—would be more pleasant than his first. Holding the stone against himself with one hand, he pushed himself up with the other. Constantine's hand came out to steady him. A moment later, Constantine withdrew it, but he did not step away.

The grizzled knight looked at the World's Ways but did not speak, only spread his hand toward the great golden doors, arrayed with stars and suns and moons, with swords and sheaves of wheat, with a crown presiding over all.

It looked more impressive than it had the last time, thought Alik. And it slid silently open before them.

Behind it, courtiers still hurried through doors and across the floor, to position themselves to either side of the throne. Many were still in disarray, straightening badges and robes of office as they took their places. King Petros himself had not quite the august attire that Alik remembered.

Constantine and Domenic bowed. Alik tried one as well; the stone made it clumsy. He blinked. He felt more tired than he ever had before in his life.

"What is the meaning of this?" said King Petros, regally.

"It means that the pirates would not have sailed to Kingsport." Alik lifted the World's Ways. "Now they will not sail anywhere at all."

Constantine reached out and firmly took the stone from his hands. Alik blinked at him. Constantine handed Domenic it and reached out to pick up Alik.

Like a baby, thought Alik. He could hear voices, and the rumble of speech in Constantine's chest, but he made out only one phrase: "My father's house."

Which still made no sense when he found himself with his face in a pillow. A full, white pillow. Swathes of white surrounded him. He even wore some kind of white tunic, and he no longer smelled of dust. He sat up.

Curtains surrounded the bed—pale embroidered deer, birds, and rabbits gamboled in riots of flowers and trees—but one curtain had been pulled back to show a white-washed room. A window showed a cityscape, in broad day, with the sun beating down on it. By the door, there stood a boy wearing a white robe with blue stripes about the wrist and throat.

The boy gasped and ran out. "He's awake, he's awake," and footsteps echoed in the corridor outside, until distance muffled the sounds. Alik scrambled from bed and went to the window.

A garden spread a floor below, filled with trees and sweet-smelling roses. Past the wall, gracious buildings spread, the highest among them the royal castle. Even from here, he could see the bustle about it.

A snort came from the doorway. A lean, grizzled man, who wore robes like the boy's, looked him up and down.

"I told them you were nothing more than tired—and you have confirmed my judgment—but you must nonetheless submit to examination."

Alik eyed him warily but went back to the bed. Slitting his throat in the night would have been easy enough. They did not mean him that ill.

The man inspected him minutely, with spells he had never seen before. Rosalba had cast some like them, but not very like. Minutes inched by, and then the man called for menservants to attend Alik.

Once they had combed his hair out and dressed him in royal blue and white, they bustled him off. Alik found himself in a long hall. Curtained windows stood to one hand, a carpet figured with flowers lay underfoot—a carpet as fine as anything the pirates had ever seized, and this one was not tracked with red dust—and mirrors, to the other hand. In the shadowy light, Alik took a dubious look at himself. The only thing that distinguished him from a pirate was that the clothing fit. And, he had to admit, the colors did not clash, or look uncomely on him.

"Ah, my young guest stirs."

The man walking down the hall wore robes of office in deep red. His hair was grizzled, but his eyes were a familiar shade of amber. The servant bowed, and the man dismissed him with a wave of his hand, not looking from Alik. The corners of his mouth quirked, causing wrinkles beside his eyes, and he bowed.

Alik, vaguely remembering what he had seen at court, bowed back.

"Come, Master Alik. In return for my son's life, I may offer you—breakfast. But then His Majesty requires your presence at the castle. They may not start without you."

Alik followed him into a room, and sat to eat. He recognized most of the dishes—he thought—at least what they were made of—but if the pirates had cooks among their captives, they still had no meals like this.

He looked up from a dish of fruit and porridge. "But—the castle—they were so busy—"

The man lifted an eyebrow. "They can ready themselves for the attack. My son and Sir Domenic can instruct them all in what they know of their encampment. But only one wizard can let them through."

The World's Ways could not be too hard to master. Not when Habrec, no wizard, had mastered it. Not when one badly trained young wizard had mastered it swiftly with no more knowledge than how to use a scrystone. . . . Alik smiled in silence and dug into the meal.

Not an hour later, the journey to the castle carried out by carriage, Alik stood before the king for a third time. The World's Ways gleamed on the table as King Petros gravely told him that on Sir Constantine's advice, they would land the forces on the beach, by the camp.

"And soon." King Petros looked, brooding, on the stone. "We have set watch for any ships, and any wind-witching, but the more pirates we catch there, the better."

Alik nodded.

"You, of course, will remain here, until word is sent that the gate should reopen, as you tried to send word of their attack. We can not risk you, you need to rest, and there is no need, really, for you to ever return."

"There are wizards there," said Alik brightly. "With—" He waved a hand. "All sorts of magical things, all the pirates' loot. My master taught me much of it." He glanced sideways. "I could help keep it innocuous. And some of it, my master wanted to be mine, after he died."

Ministers looked dismayed. Constantine and Domenic exchanged wry glances.

The king snorted. "You are a bold one."

"While I lived among the pirates, Your Majesty, nothing could be mine without my grabbing with both hands." He shrugged. "As I grabbed the World's Ways, and the lives of your knights, from the hands of the pirates."

King Petros laughed. "Your aid in dealing with such wizardry will inspire gratitude—after the battle."

Alik grinned and turned to the World's Ways. "Tell me where, and I will open the gates."

Winter's Curse

The wind swirled about the firs, in streamers of snow. Snowflakes rose as much as they fell, and elsewhere drifted along on a level, as if sauntering by.

Gareth eyed the firs—they were only trees—and looked over his shoulder to the rest of the patrol. "Nothing more! We've got to get back! Our foes won't need to fear the storm!"

The bulky form that was the captain hesitated, and Gareth's parched lips set. He wondered how many men had made the appeal before; they all had faced the captain at his words, but their hoods shielded their expressions. The captain stood, pondering, as if there were any question whether their scouting would prove useful in this storm.

The captain's shoulders slumped. "Head back!"

Will marvels never cease? thought Gareth. He slogged back, his feet sinking up to his knees with every step, and snow slipping into the boot. When he reached the others, Brand looked at him. Snow clung to the fur lining his hood.

"If Zavrien has such fearful powers," said Gareth, sharply, "why doesn't he make himself somewhere *pleasant* to live?"

A gust shoved them forward. After a minute, Brand said, his voice dejected, flat, "He can't be that powerful. Not if he needs to protect himself from us."

Gareth grimaced. The wind stung his face with snow, and he lowered his head against it to trudge on. Amazing, how eager he could be for the shelter of a few tents and still fewer fires, kept alive only by endless magic.

His hood blocked off everything except the snow before him, where the footsteps, rough shapes from the beginning, were rapidly deformed by the wind. After plodding minutes, his foot slid on ice. He clambered back to his feet and looked about.

He could not pick out another soldier in the swirling snow, or any landmark. His own footsteps vanished as swiftly as falling snow and blowing wind could muffle them. Hollows in the snow ahead no longer looked like footprints, even vaguely.

"Brand!" he shouted. The wind snatched his words. "BRAND! CAPTAIN! RUFUS!"

A narrow hand closed on his arm with a grip like steel. Even through his thick coat, he felt each distinct icy finger. His mouth abruptly dry, he turned his head.

An angular woman of pure blue, her eyes indifferent and inhuman, looked at him. Her lighting-blue hair flew on the wind, with the skirt of her thin, sleeveless dress. Gareth tried to jerk back and did not move an inch. He reached for his spear. The frost fairy stabbed at his face with her free hand. Cold surged from her fingers. The spear fell from his numb hands, and he could not move.

The frost fairy smiled. Gareth, unable to shift his eyes, stared at her and waited for the end: she had doomed him the moment she laid her hand on him.

But the cold did not extend, did not reach his heart and be his death. Nor did her smile shift.

Another creature lumbered from the veil of snow. He caught glimpses of a paler blue before an enormous hand and arm, translucent white with blue deep inside, came through his vision and closed around his waist. The giant lifted Gareth, giving him a brief glimpse of eyebrows like snowdrifts and wrinkles like icicles before throwing him over his shoulder. Gareth, unable even to blink, stared at a back like ice on a cliff-face.

"Hurry," said the frost fairy, her voice crackling. "Zavrien will not be pleased with slowness."

The giant said nothing but trudged steadily into the wind, jolting Gareth with each step. The frost fairy danced about the giant, muttering about speed. Snow flew over the giant's shoulder into Gareth's face. He blinked, sputtering. The frost fairy's attack wore off, then. He wriggled. The giant's hand tightened, and Gareth subsided. For an alarming moment, he glanced at the frost fairy, dancing on the wind, but though she spied his movements with sharp glances, she did not lay a finger on him, or even approach closer.

As if she needed to. His toes felt like chunks of ice against his feet. Gareth closed his eyes, and time blurred. God have mercy on me, he thought, and could not manage any more thought. At least he did not feel as if he were no longer cold, which would be a sign of the end—and then the thought struck, colder than the frost fairy's fingers, that he should await that moment with eagerness, as the only end of this pain.

The giant's walk went on and on, jouncing Gareth. Now and again, he felt the giant going up a slope, or down one. Then, the wind cut off as if with a knife. For a moment, he wondered if he dreamed. The giant's footsteps crunched against the ice-covered snow for a minute more; then he lifted Gareth from his shoulder.

In a field of snow, a man in a black sorcerer's robe, embroidered with coppery runes, stood with his hands clasped behind his back. His pale features held no emotion. His black hair and beard showed not a trace of snow, and though his clothing was light, he did not shiver.

"So. A soldier of the army." His melodious voice held no more emotion than his face. "The oh-so-luminous force of righteousness and truth. Eager to hunt through the north lands for the evil sorcerers."

The army, Gareth thought, had not conjured snow storms and the deaths of hundreds, leaving skeletons—and skeletons of children—scattered through the snow.

His mouth felt too leaden to move.

He could not feel the giant's grip on his arms; Zavrien would not have him much longer. Out of the depths I cry to You, o Lord, he thought, but could recall no more.

"What, nothing to say?"

Gareth swayed.

Zavrien raised his hand. Violet flames leapt from it to Gareth. Heat stabbed through his body, restoring feeling, and pain. Gareth gasped.

"Escape is not that easy," said Zavrien. He looked at the frost fairy. "Go, watch the army."

Gareth looked away as the woman flitted into the blizzard, vanishing when she reached the snowfall.

"You do not like my servants?" said Zavrien. His face contorted. "They are faithful. They are loyal. They obey me. They do not appease you with words sweet as honey and brief as dew." Gareth wondered at the passion, but if that showed in his face, Zavrien paid no heed. The wizard's breath came rapidly. "As for you, soldier, here is what I give to an invader."

His finger touched Gareth's cheek and drew straight down it.

"Ill luck follow you all your days."

His finger jabbed in other lines.

"And all who fare with you. Let it blight you, day and night, until your death."

Gareth could see a bit of black against his cheeks. He closed his eyes. Winter's Curse—he knew the mark. He should have known when the frost fairy first laid a hand on him. Why else would Zavrien have him kept alive?

But Zavrien had already turned away, and said, carelessly, "Bring him back."

The giant nodded and threw Gareth to his shoulder. The cold returned, seeping back into his body. It would not kill him in time. Soon enough, but not in time.

Perriel tried to peer through the wind-driven snow, but though her wall of air protected her from the wind, the snow all but blinded her. Those dark shapes ahead might be firs.

She shivered. The stories were too feeble. She could not have imagined this storm. If apprentices were brought here, the warnings about diabolerie would be much sharper. It might even have dissuaded Master Rodger. . . .

"Perriel!" Corry's voice rang through the wind on the wings of his spell. "The general wants us back."

"They found the rest?"

"Some." Corry emerged from the whiteness, shaking his head. "We can't risk the searchers, too."

A strand of hair had worked its way out of her braid; it poked her face. Perriel shoved it back. "We haven't found half of them!"

Corry came within the ambit of her spell, and snow no longer blew between them. His puppy-dog eyes were sorrowful. "The general's going to break the captain."

"Maybe the captain should stay behind to search."

Corry did not answer. Then, he had learned to—humor her indignation. He seldom lifted a finger to actually help.

Perriel looked away, toward the firs. "I'll just check this grove."

Corry shrugged. "I'll come with you. Two can search twice as fast."

Which meant he thought that would indeed get them back to camp earlier.

Perriel trudged through the drifts. Snow clumped in every crease in her clothing.

Corry followed, more slowly. "If we had known we would be stuck with this, we might have been less eager to deal with our master."

"Just as well we didn't know, then, isn't it?" Perriel said, tartly. She had known that Corry had followed her lead, back then, but to wish that. . . .

She wondered if Zavrien had had an apprentice who had not been eager to deal with his master, who hesitated to denounce—well, she should not think ill of the dead, who were past any judgment of *hers*. Any such apprentice had paid a stern price for his reluctance—but, she thought with a touch of acid, he had not been the only one to pay.

The firs blocked some of the wind, and much of the blowing snow. The air was almost transparent, the drifts were smaller, and a brown lump, touched with white, lay at the grove's edge—like a soldier, overcome by cold.

Perriel hurried. Snow already gathered on him, filling folds in the cloth, but a man lay there. She held a hand to his lips, and a warm breath hit her fingers. Her own breath rushed out. He looked no older than she, or Corry, was, but he was solidly built. The two of them would be hard put to carry him along.

"Corry!" She put her arms around the unconscious man. He groaned. Fearing frost-bite, Perriel turned him over. His dark hair fell over his face—his very pale face—and she shoved it aside. His eyes were still closed. On one cheek rested a sigil, black and sharp as if painted with ink. Cold from more than the weather, Perriel recognized, though she could not read, the mark. Her hand went to his cheek, trying to rub it away. The soldier jerked, but the black did not diminish.

The chilly tent was lit, and warmed a little, only by a newly lit magefire. General Ryna Iceeyes slapped her gloves into her hand. Perriel felt small, negligible, and mute. Corry knelt, silent by the cot where the soldier—Gareth—lay.

"We should not have taken you. We were not that desperate for wizards," said General Ryna. "A veteran would not have been such a fool."

Gareth murmured in his fever.

"What would the veteran have done?" Perriel said. "Left him to freeze?"

"Yes," said Ryna. A startled noise spilled from Corry's mouth, and her lip curled. "And we thought you were hard because you denounced your own master."

"Abandoning him would be murder," said Perriel, her voice sounding light in her own ears.

"He has no right to bring his curse among us!" said the general. "A plague-bearer could be forbidden the camp, and this is worse than a plague!"

"And," said a captain, "it would have been kinder. Freezing to death is not that hard a way to die."

Perriel took a step backwards. Her voice grew plaintive. "Can't the curse be lifted? The Spell-Breaker. . . ."

"No one has," said Ryna. The wind buffeted the tent. "No one under Winter's Curse has lived long enough for many attempts to be made."

Corry rose. His dark eyes were troubled. "If he is dangerous. . . ."

"He's ill," Perriel said. Her gaze fell from Ryna's face, came back, and fell again. "The spells work quickly. If we cured him tonight and left him in the morning, he might—"

Ryna looked at her in cold silence.

"I'll stay the night with him," Perriel said.

"I could make you come away," said Ryna, softly.

"She's very hard to move once she's set on a path," said Corry.

Perriel opened her mouth to protest—she had never insisted on anything but reporting Master Rodger's diabolerie, which could have *killed* them—but Ryna shrugged, and she closed her mouth. Tending Gareth came first. She could quibble with Corry later.

"We have nothing against him, child," said the general. "I know that some have spoken of him as promising, and it is a misfortune to lose him. But we will. All that matters is how many he takes with him." She turned to Corry. "Come with me, Corry. I wish to speak with you."

The tent darkened; falling snow clumped on the canvas, and the night approached. At least the light spell's steady warmth had managed to accumulate, taking the edge from the chill. Perriel studied the sigil—no paint, but an illusion on top of the curse. It was always harder to break a spell under an illusion; the illusion affected not only the sight, but a wizard's ability to discern what manner of curse it hid. She had seen that before, but never so masterful a concealment.

She supposed that holding the lands bound in winter showed a little skill at wizardry.

When, in the darkness, Corry came with supper, she asked for her spell-books. He glanced, frightened, at Gareth, but returned with the books—shoving them into the tent even more quickly than he had the supper.

Gareth occasionally rambled, but his sleep calmed. Perriel sat with her chosen book propped up against her knees for long, fruitless hours, but finally slept. A thought dawned on her just as the blankets grew warm: that Zavrien had found Gareth argued that he knew where the army was.

Briefly, Perriel thought of rousing, and warning the army. She turned over. A bitter draft touched her neck, and she huddled into the blankets again. Ryna, being a general, probably had thought of it already. Further proof, in her eyes, that Perriel was unfit for the army—thinking a wizard new to war could lecture a veteran—and rousing her from sleep to do it, no doubt.

Perriel drifted off to a sleep.

Light suffused the tent through the canvas, as if it were midmorning rather than dawn. Silence pervaded the camp. The storm had died down, but this was more than the want of the wind's blast.

Perriel tasted something bitter in her mouth.

Gareth coughed.

Perriel, oblivious to the cold, threw back the blankets, scrambled to her sock-clad feet, and ran to the door. She could recognize landmarks from when they had first camped here, when the snow had first approached, but the sun, half way to zenith, shone on glittering snow. Wind had obliterated every trace of the camp, leaving not even any hollows in the flatness before her. Chill attacked her fingers and nose, but Perriel could not move away. She could not have slept this late. If nothing else, the noise of breaking camp would have woken her.

Gareth shifted behind her. She let in cold on her patient as well as herself—not a virtue in a nurse.

Perriel let the flap fall from her fingers, though she felt so stunned that even that motion was difficult. She wondered if she would have defended Gareth, had she known that they would desert her, as well. General Ryna had threatened to force her— and Corry had argued against it. Had he convinced them that she would prove dangerous? Her fingers twisted together. She had known him for many years, as a child, as a fellow apprentice; she could not swear that he would not have. He might even have known it when he brought her dinner.

"Lord, have mercy on us," she whispered. She drew a deep breath. "Christ, have mercy on us. Lord, have mercy on us. St.

Michael, Archangel, defend us in battle. St. David, pray for us. St. Casper, pray for us. St. Melchior, pray for us. St. Balthazar, pray for us." She swallowed. The two of them camped alone in a wilderness of endless winter—of an evil wizard's endless, enchanted winter. "St. Jude, pray for us."

Gareth groaned, startling her. "Water," he begged, his eyes still closed.

Just as well she had not known, then, Perriel decided virtuously. She turned slowly from the door and trudged over to their supplies. More had been brought in over the night: bread, cheese, dried meat, even some dried fruit. It was the same dried, hard, and tasteless meals they had always eaten in Zavrien's lands, but it would take long for them to starve on this.

Perriel's eyebrows rose. General Ryna must have had a conscience about abandonment. She picked up the water bottle. Though not much of one.

She propped Gareth up and held the water to his mouth, holding her hand steady by main force until Gareth stopped drinking. He slumped against her arm; she had to fight to not let him drop but lower him gently. He looked pitifully young.

If he did not survive—she lacked the winter lore to survive in this wilderness. Carefully, she capped the bottle, trying to suppress her hands' trembling. General Ryna knew how little she knew about the land.

Feeling pitifully young, Perriel managed only to put the bottle back before she collapsed against her cot, burying her face against the blankets.

Gareth's throat burned—again? he thought, vaguely. The dead silence made him wonder what had happened to his ears. He opened his eyes a crack and saw only canvas, with the sunlight behind it.

A low song came from behind him: a woman singing children's rhymes under her breath. He could not be deaf then.

He rolled over. A woman stood over packs of supplies with her back to him, her straw blond hair falling down her back in two braids. Gareth wondered who she was and swallowed. Pain stabbed through his throat. "Water," he pled.

The song cut off. A second later, she bent over him, putting her arm around his shoulders. He tried to sit without her help, but even that effort made him realize his weakness. The woman, her face set, held the water to his mouth. Gareth gulped, and his throat eased. The woman tilted the bottle, and Gareth drank more carefully, for fear of spilling it. The woman's pale, heart-shaped face was still strange to him, though he vaguely remembered something about water. A second later, his swallow got him only half a mouthful; he had drained the bottle. The woman pulled it back and lowered him to the cot.

No shapes outside cast shadows on the canvas, and he could still hear nothing. "What happened to the army?"

"They left." Her blue eyes met his, glanced at his cheek for a second, and looked back.

He let out his breath. He had asked the wrong question. He should have asked why he yet received shelter, water, and nursing. The woman had supplies from the army. She had to know. Someone would have told her if nothing else.

"Who are you?" he said.

"A fool." Her mouth twitched. "My name is Perriel. I am also a wizard."

The room was tiny, with a single, round window, but the bed was her familiar bed, with the blue quilt that her mother had made for her. Perriel smiled. What a dream she had had.

The breeze carried the smell of baking bread. She would have it with honey this morning, before Master Rodger reviewed the light spell with her. She pushed back the blanket.

Cold washed in, and Perriel blinked at the tent. Her patient slept, across the tent. She dragged in a deep breath and nearly froze her lungs. She hugged the blankets over her, and tears streaked hotly across her face. What a dream she had had, indeed.

Swirls of snow, like infant ghosts, ran over the plain. Slate-gray clouds covered the sky. Perriel shivered in the wind but could not step inside. After a week in the tent, with Gareth asleep most of the time, the occasional effort of melting snow over the magefire did not exhaust her, she had few spells she could practice, and even the frozen waste had some allure.

Gareth was asleep and, she decided, well enough to leave for a time. Her heart lightened at the thought. She pulled her heavy coat over the lighter one she wore in the tent and laced it against the wind. With a final glance to be sure Gareth did not stir, Perriel pulled up her hood and set out into the cold. Her feet sank into the snow, but no higher than her ankles. She walked briskly, the wind at her back.

The clouds turned the daylight into a brilliant white glow, and left the snowdrifts almost shadowless, where snow hissed as it poured before the wind. Perriel's toes, fingers, and nose tingled with cold, but it was such a relief to walk. Every now and then, she glanced behind herself to pick out the tent, but she could not stop walking, though the tent was nothing more than a dot on the snow.

Firs appeared ahead of her. Perriel stepped without thinking and slid on a patch of ice, landing on her face. She scrambled up and tried to brush the snow off. Some fell back, but the glittering crystals stuck. Then, she had had her walk. She turned.

The wind struck her in the face. Perriel blinked. The snow suddenly no longer rose in little swirls but in eddies, growing larger even as she watched. She had never seen it rise so quickly before.

She could still see the tent. After a glance at the distance, she stopped to cast the shield of air. The chill leached heat from her body as she wove the spell, but the stillness as the spell went up felt like warmth in itself. She started back.

Gusts of wind shoved the shield, again and again. The tent grew larger, but no more distinct. The air behind the shield, though calm, was still cold and would leach warmth from her. Perriel's mouth set as pushing against the snow grew harder. A misplaced foot slid against ice, twisted, and threw her into a snow bank. Perriel floundered to her feet again and blinked. Snow clung to her eyelashes. Her feet felt like chunks of ice, and her fingers were numb. She pulled her fingers from her gloves' fingers and tucked them into her palms to warm them.

Snow swirled, hiding the tent. Her mouth set, she trudged onward, picking out the shape as it appeared between gusts but still walked when it was hidden.

A pale face, surrounded by silvery gray hair, appeared in the whiteness and smiled. Perriel blinked. The smile deepened. The woman behind it, dressed in a sky-blue gown and cloak, emerged from the snow. She twirled, the silvery fringe on her clothing flying, and stopped to hold out her hand to Perriel. The wind sank, and with it the snow, letting her see again. All about the plain, frost fairies danced over the drifts.

Perriel blinked again. Her legs and arms felt like lead.

The frost fairy's voice slid through the shield. "Come, dance. Warm yourself."

That made sense. Moving would warm her. She held out her hand, and the frost fairy took it. Perriel felt warmer and smiled.

The other frost fairies, beaming, gathered around her. Perriel tossed her head. Her hood fell back. Her blond hair spilled out—almost as pale as the fairies', thought Perriel.

Gareth rolled over and pushed back the covers. The chilly air in the tent was more bracing than unpleasant. He looked about and realized the woman—Perriel—was gone. He felt a cold weight in his stomach. The curse might have struck her. It did not take long for it to act.

The wind was not loud, but vague noises came from outside, like footsteps on packed snow. For a moment, his heart seemed to stop. Then it hammered in his chest.

He forced himself to his feet—easier than he would have guessed—donned his boots, and went over to the door, grabbing his coat on the way. Pushing open the flap sent icy air, and a swirl of snowflakes, into his face. Perriel stood not five paces away, her blond hair bare. A frost fairy held the wizard's hand as she leached the warmth from Perriel's body. More than a dozen frost fairies gathered around. Their pale skirts of green, blue, and white swirled, and they smiled in wolfish anticipation.

His heart hammered. Once, he had seen a man who had danced with the frost fairies. The corpse had been frozen solid.

The fairies danced, their cloaks and hair lifting on the wind. The fairy holding Perriel's hand lifted one foot. Perriel smiled, stiffly, and followed the fairy into the dance, moving with the clumsiness of deep chill. Nonetheless, the graceful fairies let her join hands with them.

Gareth's hand tightened on the flap. The dance flitted before the tent, Perriel being drawn now closer, as if they taunted her with the nearness of safety (though she showed no sign of awareness), now further away.

A stride from the tent, a frost fairy released Perriel's hand.
Perriel turned to the next. Gareth jumped from the tent and
snagged her around the waist. She jumped, startled, but did not
fight—she showed no signs of recognition, any more than she
had for the tent. His mouth set, Gareth hauled her back. The
snow and wind swirled faster as the fairies turned their attention
on him, and icy pellets stung his face. The nearest frost fairy took
a step toward him, but Gareth felt the dead air, where the tent
cut off the wind, and hauled Perriel within.

A piercing wail rose from the frost fairies. He shivered,
wishing he had fastened his coat before the rescue, but Perriel did
not shiver. Her body had given up on warmth. His panic
deepening, Gareth pulled the tent door shut and pulled off his
coat. The air, chilly even inside, struck at him, but that he had to
endure.

"Take your clothing off," he told Perriel. "It's not keeping you
warm."

She blinked, looked down, and tugged at her coat, but the
lacings slipped through her fingers. With an oath, Gareth
crossed the tent. Perriel blinked occasionally as he stripped her
down her shift. Damn Zavrien anyway, Gareth thought. I will
not surrender her to him this easily.

"Oh, join us!" called a sweet and lovely voice from outside.
Gareth's mouth set. I should have warned her before, he
thought; we lost men to frost fairies every year—even men who
were not cursed.

Pulling off Perriel's gloves showed that her fingers, though red
with cold, were not frost-bitten. He pulled them into his hands;
they felt like ice. The tent grew colder by the moment as the
frost fairies lingered about it.

"Sit on my bed," Gareth said. Perriel glanced between the
cots, as if trying to realize which one was which, but obeyed
without being told. He pulled her boots off and pushed her
under the blankets, which, fortunately, still held warmth from his

body. Her eyes closed. The frost fairies' voices faded, but the tent grew colder. Gareth stripped his own clothing off, down his shirt. Without a fire, he had only one way to warm Perriel.

She barely stirred as he slid into the bed beside her and pulled the blankets over their heads. Her feet and hands, against him, were like chunks of ice. Gareth scowled. Most victims of Winter's Curse died because of monsters. He pulled her hands against his chest, and Perriel cried out in pain as warmth stripped away numbness. She started to shiver, and Gareth breathed a sigh of relief. After a moment, he reached out to grabbed their coats, and add them to the blankets about them.

Long hours later, with Perriel warm and asleep, Gareth brooded. General Ryna should not have to abandoned anyone whom she could protect to the tender mercies of Zavrien's curse. His hand traced his cheek again. If Perriel had insisted—she was only one woman, wizard or not, and could still have been forced away. By the other wizards, if need be. If they could not stand up to this Perriel, who had not even finished her apprenticeship, what good could they be against Zavrien?

Perriel's magefire burned in the tent, radiating heat without light. The midnight outside left the tent like pitch. Gareth stared across the room to Perriel's cot anyway.

"We have supplies to reach the Spell-Breaker," said Perriel, swathed in blankets. "A powerful wizard. He lives not that far outside Zavrien's lands."

"No wizard of the army ever lifted Zavrien's curse," said Gareth. "How could a wizard who never fought him?"

Perriel's blankets shifted. "Most powerful wizards aren't for hire. They don't go in for diabolerie, either, so the army does not fight them. They consider it. . . cheating."

Gareth snorted. Of all the things he might call dealing with devils, "cheating" was the last. "That's all they think of it?"

"The Art," said Perriel lightly, "is a life-long study. Not a hobby or a jest. The more powerful a wizard is, the more he has studied. A wizard interested in other things will never be as powerful as one who is not. The army, diabolerie—they are other things." She shifted again, her blankets rustling. "Every Epiphany, the priest would mention in his sermon that doubtlessly other wise men—other magi—had seen the star, but only Casper, Melchior, and Balthazar thought it worth leaving their studies for."

Gareth stared up, as if he could see the canvas overhead.

"There are wizards," said Perriel, more dryly, "who have let Zavrien's lands swamp them. Whose studies have continued unabated, when surrounded by snow."

Gareth looked through the dark with narrowed eyes. She had undercut her own point. "Wouldn't they find lifting the curse something—different?"

"The Spell-Breaker studies the breaking of spells—and the Winter's Curse would be a new spell for him." Gareth heard little conviction in her voice. Then she lowered her voice. "We can't stay here. The frost fairies know where we are."

She was right there.

Gareth thought of letting the creatures kill them—and revolted. One thing to suffer under a curse, and another to grovel before it.

General Dirk had killed himself rather than bring the curse on the army, he remembered. He turned his face into his pillow, as if he could hide from that memory.

Perriel's voice drifted across the tent. "They use our spells for the maps, to determine distance and direction. And I have a map. I can see that we do not go in circles."

He could kill himself getting her out of Zavrien's lands. Perhaps *she* could escape.

Clouds of charcoal gray billowed in the west; it was evening, but light vanished more swiftly than that alone would bring. They needed to find shelter, Perriel knew, but when they should trudge onward, she could not stop looking about at things that would never provide enough. Ragged tree trunks, torn to shreds, with snow and ice caught in the gaps. Chunks of wood sprawled, here and there breaking through the snow, as if some giant smashed the trees—which, she supposed, was possible.

"They exploded," said Gareth.

"What?"

"The trees froze and exploded," said Gareth. "I've gathered firewood from forests like this. And we—" His face was grim. Suddenly, he no longer seemed her own age. "The armies avoid forests, for fear Zavrien will attack with like cold."

He walked on, and she, still considering, scrambled alongside him. "That means—that means we can take no shelter from intact trees—that was why we, the army, did not camp near the firs—"

His mouth twitched. "*We* can take shelter by them. The army could not, but—" He pointed at his cheek. "Zavrien does not plague the cursed with more magic. He lets the curse take its course."

Her mouth pursed. "What if new spells are not needed? It is winter, it grows cold—"

He shook his head. "His spells cause the winter, it does not act naturally and turn bitter cold on occasion." He glanced at her. "And the frost fairies can't make it that cold, either."

For small blessings, give thanks—perhaps when they found a grove that could still shelter two wanderers. These could not.

Past the ruined trees, he picked out a hill. "We'll camp here."

She hurried to help him with the tent. The storm moved quickly; before they were done, it began to rain. Gareth scowled. "Worse than snow. Get inside."

Perriel looked at him in surprise, even as she obeyed.

He followed her in. "It will freeze. And then it will be ice all over."

Perriel remembered the few patches she had slipped on, hidden here and there. If everywhere was ice. . . . Her mouth shut.

"You'll have to warm the tent, so that it does not ice over," said Gareth. "Too much snow will fall off when it rises too high. Too much ice will cling, and grow heavy, and then—" He spread his hands.

She cast the spell.

The cloudless sky was brilliant and intensely blue. The oaks glittered like diamonds from the ice that encased their branches. A breeze sent dazzling chips of ice, and branches entombed in them, splattering. Gareth shifted his pack. The ice storm had covered the snow with a crust, but every step broke through with a crunch. It could be much worse—even if he and Perriel had both fallen more than once.

"We can camp again if you're tired," Perriel said. White clouds puffed from her mouth with her words. "Better than letting you sicken again." She gestured to a grove ahead, dark even in the snow. "The firs would give us some shelter."

Perriel, perhaps, was not used to the marches. He nodded. Whatever she dreamed of wizards and help against the curse, it wasn't as if they had to go somewhere. She hiked up the straps of her pack on her shoulders and plodded on.

Beneath the firs, the snow sank to a blanket on the ground, peppered with golden fir needles. The trees cut off a wind Gareth had not been conscious of.

A cluster of rocks stuck through the snow and fir needles. Perriel stared.

"What is it?" Gareth asked.

Perriel's hand pointed the line that the rocks ran in, no higher than her knee in any place, with loose stone to either side. "Stone wall. Probably from a farm. This was all farmland once."

Gareth gave her a sideways look and spoke coolly. "There are stone walls about here. We've seen a number over the years." Often with skeletons huddled in the lee. "Not collapsed piles of rocks."

Her hand swept the air. "Those were farms when Zavrien struck. This—must have been abandoned before then. Years before. But—" She scowled as if looking at something. "If I remember the map right, these hills were not good for farming. Many farmers abandoned them after roads improved, and more food could be brought in."

He did not dispute it. Walls, in his experience, meant there might be shelter nearby and not much else.

Perriel blinked. "Haven't you heard the story? I thought that most of the soldiers had fought Zavrien for as long as they had been in the army."

Gareth's mouth set. He would not admit that it had never occurred to him that there was much of a story. Zavrien was there, and they fought him.

"Of course," Perriel said, reflectively, "I heard the story in my apprenticeship, and not since I joined the army. I doubt it would help fight him."

Gareth felt a snap of resentment. It was not his fault that he was no wizard. But Perriel was looking about.

"Let's find the farmhouse—that'll be better shelter—and I'll tell you."

Gareth choked his temper down. It was not Perriel's fault, either. And if they quarreled, she had nowhere to go.

Perriel stepped over the ruined wall and walked out from teh firs. "Once upon a time, there was a city here—I forget its name. You would never have seen it, or its ruins. They're the center of Zavrien's lands, the very heart, and his stronghold. But it was a thriving city, surrounded by farmlands, filled with merchants, with many wizards."

Another line of scattered stone broke through the snow. Perriel stepped over it.

"Zavrien was a wizard and a lord in it. Some other lord used an arcane law to cheat Zavrien, and Zavrien conjured an imp to plague the other lord—just an imp, not some great fiend."

The wind came over the field, and snow hissed before it. Perriel pulled her coat more tightly about herself. "In that hollow, there?"

Gareth grunted with surprise. A chimney stood, with three walls about it and a half-intact roof. "Better shelter than we've had for a while." They plugged through the snow.

Perriel went on as if she had not broken into her own story. "The other lord found out who had conjured the imp. Zavrien summoned a demon to protect himself from justice. The demon taught him to summon up a storm that would ward them off." Her mouth quirked. "The storm went further than Zavrien intended. No one for many miles around survived, except Zavrien himself."

Gareth remembered skeletons, littered about: grown men and women, children, little babies.

She reached the opening in the farmhouse. "Ever since then, he's lived in the ruins and conjured up spirits to do his work, and to protect him from paying for what he did."

"And add to what he will pay if he ever must," said Gareth, dryly.

"Oh, yes," said Perriel. "The land under snow's grown because it's safer that way."

She plunged into the house. Gareth followed. A thin layer of snow—even thinner than under the firs—covered the dirt floor. With a sigh of relief, he let his pack slide off.

Perriel unslung her own and worked her fingers as if they were stiff. After a minute, she moved them in familiar gestures: the magefire. Blue light popped into the air over Perriel's hands, flickering with aquamarine and violet. The fire cast multi-colored shadows across her face.

She grinned at his intent gaze. Gareth blushed and looked away; though this was the first time she had caught him, he had stared every time.

"Like magic?" said Perriel.

"Yes," said Gareth, trying to keep his longing from his voice. He stepped closer to warm his hands.

"Parents couldn't afford an apprenticeship?"

Gareth said, "I was an infant oblate."

Perriel's thoughts warred in her face: what to say in consolation—if anything could console. Gareth looked away. Many parents who offered their children were too poor to feed them. Others offered their children to atone for their sins or to keep the children from impeding the sins. His shoulders hunched. The army ought not to take such children, but how could they refuse any help with the wizards? Even with all the infant oblates, the army never had enough men.

"Did—do you know what kind of wizard you wanted to become?" Perriel said, with determined cheerfulness.

Gareth blinked. He had tried to not even think of it; few soldiers even of those who showed promise were sent off to learn magic. "Wizards are wizards, aren't they?"

"Oh, no," Perriel said. "Some master spells of knowledge, some of form and motion, some of weather. . . ."

"Like Zavrien?"

"Not before the demon taught him," said Perriel. "Perhaps that's why he didn't know how strong it was—some of disenchantment, some of illusion."

As he had had any chance to become any kind of wizard. "No, I did not know."

Silence fell for a minute.

"I could teach you a spell or two," Perriel said. "It might prove useful."

Ever hopeful Perriel. Gareth pointed at his cheek. "It would go awry—somehow—and likely kill us."

Perriel's eyebrows went up. "If our plight is that desperate, it would be quicker and cleaner than many other ways to die."

Gareth looked away. She still did not realize how dire their plight was.

Perriel sighed. She crouched to open her pack. "I wonder how the army fares."

"Not well," snarled a voice behind them. Perriel whirled. Gareth looked up. Brand, his expression fierce, glared at him as if Gareth were a wild animal and not, only weeks ago, his comrade-in-arms. His face was caked with blood; his clothing was grimy, tattered, and blood-stained. Gareth took a step forward.

"I saw the light, I should have known it would have to be you two monsters. . . ." Brand's chapped lips pulled back from his teeth. "You should know, Gareth. General Dirk knew what to do. You had his example, but you brought your curse on us."

Perriel gestured aimlessly, her voice protesting and light. Her gaze went between them. "He was unconscious; Corry and I brought him. . . ."

Brand's smile grew more feral. "That fool Corry should have known—Winter's Curse. . . the first to fall." Perriel gasped. "But not the last." He leaned forward, toward her, his voice deepening. "And you brought this on us. General Ryna was right to leave you; it's not *his* fault, but *yours*."

Perriel, deathly pale, stepped backwards. "Hold him off!"

Brand snarled and lunged, knocking Gareth sprawling. The ground hit like another blow, and Gareth fought for breath. Perriel stood somewhere behind him; he had to buy her time. Brand loomed over him. Gareth kicked, unbalancing him, and scrambled up in the brief respite.

"You wretched. . . ." Brand's words froze in mid-sentence, his face as contorted and immobile as a gargoyle's.

Moments inched by. Finally, Gareth turned.

Perriel, breathing hard, lowered her hands and spoke, very lightly. "That should hold him." Her voice grew even lighter. "Did you know him?"

"He was a soldier in the army, in my company. He was my friend." Gareth stepped back. At least, he had called him his friend, and now— "Is he dead?"

"I could release him." Her mouth contorted in derision. "The spell will wear off in hours." The wind whistled around the farmhouse. She shuddered. "What disaster befell the army?"

Gareth's eyes closed at the thought of marching on. "We have to leave. The only safety we could find here would be to slit Brand's throat."

Perriel shoved the magefire toward the immobile man with jerky hands. "He can not move, but he can still freeze. We have to leave this."

"It could attract—things," Gareth said. Half-described monsters flooded his thoughts.

Perriel's mouth set in unhappy lines. "It attracted him—but we can hope that the spell wears off first. The one mercy of this winter is that there are few wild beasts about." She slung on her own pack, her movements convulsive.

Gareth reached for his pack. "Who was Corry?"

Her voice was light and distant. "We were neighbors as children, and our parents apprenticed us to the same wizard. When the wizard. . . died before our apprenticeship was done, we took service with the army together."

And now, thought Gareth, he was dead. Her eyes were suspiciously bright, but she was not actually weeping.

"They must have been attacked not long after they left us." The words plopped out, without significance. "Not a day or two, or the morning we marched out, but we did not rest that long. For him to catch up to us, they had to have—" He shook his head.

She flinched and glanced sideways at him. "Was he tracking us?"

"The soldiers who survived must have scattered over the landscape. One was bound to happen on us." If there were enough alive to spread that far. He wondered how many men he had known had survived. Perhaps none beside Brand. He shuddered. He knew that his eyes, unlike Perriel's, were dry.

Perriel straightened her pack and spoke woodenly. "We have to find a wizard who can lift the curse."

As the farm vanished behind them, Perriel said, "Who was General Dirk?"

"He was the third or fourth to fall under the curse. He killed himself."

"That would be a sin," Perriel said. Despite her efforts, her voice was thin. Gareth looked away. She scowled, studying his face. Then, she snapped, "Don't even think it," and managed to put some strength into *that*.

Gareth blinked.

"Abandon me in the middle of the howling wilderness? Under a curse? Promise me that."

Gareth's voice was lifeless. "Some of Dirk's companions when he was cursed survived."

"You've seen how helpless I am among the snows." She drew a deep breath. "I never faced blizzards before this campaign. I would have died among the frost fairies. . . ."

Gareth's face was unmoved.

"You can not mean to abandon me!" She felt the tears starting to her eyes. She was panicking herself, she realized, but she did not even try to blink them away. Shameless, shameless, she told herself.

Gareth looked away. "I promise," he whispered.

She let her breath out slowly. It would, she told herself virtuously, help keep him alive as well.

Two days later, they sat beneath a cliff-face, contemplating the prospect of snowfall. Gareth eyed the clouds. Though they were no more than ash gray, he declared, "No farther."

It was not yet noon. Perriel did not argue. She eyed the clouds, hoping it would reveal whatever differences Gareth had seen, but then turned aside. The cliff would shelter them as long as the wind did not turn.

She glanced at Gareth. "I could show you the magefire. It would help pass the time."

His glance was sidelong. "I could burn down the tent."

"We will set the tent up and put my magefire inside it, to warm it. Then do it a few strides away. That way, we will not go crazy from boredom. We could sit about for *hours*." She smiled, mischievously. "That was how I wandered into the frost fairies' reach; I was bored."

Gareth glowered, but said, "It'll pass the time, I suppose." He slung his pack along the stone and reached for the tent.

Perriel reached for the canvas. Theory before practice would sort out whether Gareth truly wanted to be a wizard. "Actually,

we do not *make* the magefire. A wizard can not *make* anything.
He can only transform or transport."

"And which is magefire?" said Gareth, his voice sullen.

"Transport," said Perriel. "You snatch some sunlight from the
sky and pop it through a hole."

Gareth scowled in thought.

"My old master used to say that a wizard who claimed to *make*
anything was a diabolist," said Perriel. "Because he was lying, and
the Devil is the father of lies." Her old master. Her lightness slid
away. She wondered if she should have told Gareth that Master
Rodger had been executed for diabolerie, and that she and Corry
had turned him in. Corry. She swallowed. If he had not feared
being abandoned by the army—why, Corry might be alive to that
day.

Perriel sniffed. She could *not* teach Gareth while wailing.
And if she had nothing to do, she would dwell on Corry's death
until she went insane.

Gareth studied her. When she tugged on the canvas, he
moved to raise it. Minutes later, Perriel stood in the tent and
summoned up the magefire—the dark magefire, which brought
only heat and no light, and could attract neither monsters nor
soldiers. That done, she turned to Gareth. "Let's go."

Gareth raised an eyebrow, but followed her out into the
snowfall.

"What you need to conjure up is a hole between here and the
sky."

Gareth glanced up. Snow started to drift toward the ground.

"Past the clouds," she said, as snow clung to her arms. "The
sun never stops shining up there. Not even at night—you must
just pick the right portion of the sky." Laboriously, she went
through the incantation and gesture. It was the first spell a
wizard learned, which meant she had learned it long ago herself.
The snowfall had thickened before she was done.

"Now, try it." Her heart beat faster. Wizards taught this as the first spell because failure seldom proved dangerous, but Gareth did lie under Winter's Curse. . . .

He lifted his hands. She did not dare say anything before him, or even step back, to perturb his confidence. The incantation came sharply through his teeth, and a dot of red and orange, like a coal from the center of the fire, or a fire opal from a dragon's hoard, hung in midair. It gleamed, brilliantly.

Gareth's jaw dropped.

The light vanished, but he did not stop staring until his gaze went down to his hands.

Perriel smiled. Her own first one had not lasted much longer.

"The rest," she said, "is practice."

Gareth slowly turned his head to look at her. Her smile broadened. He smiled back and looked, for a moment, younger than she was. A foolish thought considered that Gareth was more handsome than Corry, or many men in the army, or living by her old master's. She strangled it—lust had no place when they wrestled with curses and death—and the snow fell more thickly even over the last few moments.

"Try it again," she said. "It won't strain you for some time. And it would be be wise to have it ready."

A week later, the noon sky was the purest of blue, and the light glancing from the snow, almost painfully bright, but a gust hit them with powdery snow as they hurried behind a hillside.

Perriel slapped her hands against her legs to knock the snow off. "I think we're nearing the borders of Zavrien's lands."

"We'd need more luck for that than I expect."

The curse, thought Perriel, does not make him make these delightful retorts. His practice with the magefire, all week, had given him more skill than she had had after studying that long.

Last night he had even warmed their tent, alone, without disaster.

Gareth looked over the snow ahead, his gaze traveling to two hillocks ahead. "Soldiers from the army," he said, his voice low, pointing at the blood-stained and ragged group.

Her anger sank to forlornness. Even she could see at a glance that no one had seen them yet, but they could not stay even in the shelter of the hillside. They moved back into the wind. Gareth looked as grim as death. Perriel's head bowed. She trudged on, staring at the blank whiteness before her feet. They might never reach the Spell-Breaker, however easily she had urged the path on Gareth.

They climbed a hill, and she carefully heeded Gareth's directions, before the soldiers could see them against the sky. And then they slogged onward. Their shadows lengthened on the snow before them.

She slowly summoned up Master Rodger's lessons. She had first thought of the Spell-Breaker because of the aptness of his skill, but the age had other wizards of great power. She had known—she had told Gareth—that some wizards lived in Zavrien's lands. . . she laid her knowledge against their path.

"There's a wizard," she said slowly, "who lives near here, called the Wizard of the Golden Tower." No excitement in her voice, she noted. "She is very powerful—and the Golden Tower's closer than the Spell-Breaker." She turned her face toward him. "It's in Zavrien's lands."

"You," said Gareth dryly, "are the one who knows anything about wizards."

She stopped in her tracks to look at him. He raised an eyebrow. After a minute, she told him how they had to change their path.

"And you're doing well enough with the magefire," she added. "This evening, I start to teach you the map spells."

"Will we have time to learn them before the tower?" said Gareth dryly.

"You know how storms can blow up without warning. And how deep the snow can get, to slow us even in fair weather."

The evening sky gleamed pink and yellow over the mountains. Gareth inspected the landscape for shelter. Perriel's head was bowed, her blond hair straying from her braids to loop over her cheeks. His mouth tightened; she never admitted to exhaustion. Even though there was no point in her pressing herself in the foolish hope that this wizard of the Golden Tower would manage what generations of army wizards had failed in.

"We had best camp soon," he said. "Find shelter before the light fails."

"We could find the Golden Tower before nightfall," said Perriel, though her voice held little hope. He looked out over the slopes. Snow, snow, snow—here a tree, there a cliff-face—no sign of habitation—but much that could hide a building, even a tower.

"How far?" He had yet to fully master the mapping spells, he had to rely on her—and her sunny hope of finding it easily.

"I think. . . ." said Perriel, straightening. Then she hurried forward, her gaze on a slope ahead. He followed, and she turned to him and pointed.

A golden orange tower perched on the mountain side, over a frozen lake. One pitch black window looked down on them, just visible at this distance. Loose gray shale surrounded it, the flat stones ready to fall at a touch.

His eyes narrowed. He could not make out a door, and—. "No road to it," he said dourly.

Perriel laughed, as merrily as birdsong in spring. "A wizard powerful enough to raise the curse needs no road." And then she ran off, her braids and loose hairs flying behind her.

Wizards, Gareth thought. Half-formed thoughts of what protective enchantments the wizard could have waiting for them drifted through his mind—the monsters distorted by his ignorance. He sighed. With the curse, something had to lurk in their path, but she would never believe him.

"Gareth!" Perriel stood half way up the slope, her hands on her hips. Gareth climbed after. He bent his head to watch his footing; the ultimate in irony would be for the curse to break their ankles at the doorstep of a wizard who could help them.

A choked cry came from ahead of him. A glow of gold surrounded Perriel, freezing her in mid-stride. His foot landed on an unsteady slab, and he barely kept to his feet, but he could not look away. He should never have let her get so far ahead.

The gold shimmered. Gareth tried to jump to her aid, taking no heed for his footing. His feet slid out from under him, and gold suffused his vision, all but blinding him. But he did not fall to the stones he could barely see below him. He could not even hear himself breathing.

Gloom surrounded him, and he fell again. He threw his hands out and caught himself on a flagstone floor. The dark gray slabs were cold and rough against his hands, and something scrabbled on the stone beside him. With a grunt, he pushed himself up. Perriel, her feet braced, already stood beside him, staring ahead at the walls; her face was white. Gareth dragged in a deep breath. The still air felt warmer than outside. Perhaps it was warmer.

A door, beside them, opened on a stairway. A single window looked white by contrast to the walls and floor. Gareth pushed his hood back. In the center stood a table, thick as a butcher's board and of dark brown oak. Past it, the cabinets glinted with glass or metal, and on an abundance of shelves, books overflowed.

A wizard stood behind the table. Dove gray robes swathed her to the floor, making her almost invisible among the shadows. There might be silvery runes on the robes; he could not be sure. Her hood hid the face behind, but Gareth could feel the eyes watching him.

Her voice was colder than the winter. "What brings two from the army to the door I do not have?"

Perriel flinched.

The wizard's voice rolled on. "The captains of that army know that I have no door to my tower. And why I do not. Why did they not warn you?"

"The army did not send us," said Gareth. He swallowed, trying to clear the hoarseness from his words. "The army wants nothing to do with us. We came seeking aid to lift a curse."

He could hear his heart hammer in the silence. Perriel had managed to give him some of her hope. But to reach that hope, he would have to show her what he wanted. He turned his head, revealing the mark.

Silence fell. He swallowed. She could cast them out as easily as she brought them in, and they could break their necks in the fall if she did. Powerful though she was, she might be wiser if she did, leaving them alone to suffer the curse.

"I have heard of Winter's Curse before," the wizard murmured, "but never seen it."

Perriel bit her lip. Gareth swallowed again. She had not said that she had no interest in such matters.

"Interesting." The wizard spread the word over several moments. Her voice sounded almost faraway, and her eyes unfocused. "Zavrien has wrought this spell with all his power—and disguised it well. I will need days to unravel it."

Gareth's heart slowed like a racer reaching the finish line.

The wizard tilted her head. "Have you eaten, lately?"

"We have supplies," Perriel said, weakly.

The wizard pointed at the door, though her hand was still invisible beneath the gray cloth. "The kitchen is at the bottom of the stairs. I must prepare."

Perriel scurried. Gareth followed her, to stairs even more gloomy than the room. He thought of magefire, considered the wizard upstairs, and decided the stairs were well-lit enough.

Here and there, as they descended, doors stood—solid oak, bound with dark metal—but Gareth did not even wonder what lay behind them. They had no locks, he noted, with a bit of amusement.

Halfway down, a window's glow lightened the stairway. "I wonder," said Perriel, "if she knows what she looks like."

Gareth blinked. "How could she?"

"Wizards can forget everything. My old master. . . ." Perriel hesitated. "Corry and I had to roust him out of his books for our lessons."

"Admirable lack of vanity if so," he said, dryly.

The stairs looped around the tower twice. Their footsteps resounded, and then the kitchen opened out. Cabinets stood to one side. Its hearth was big enough to hold an ox, but cold. Though soot marked the stones, no firewood stood beside it, and no ash within it. The only light came from a window that opened to the slate-covered hillside. Perriel looked out and said, "Door or no door, we could have climbed through that."

Gareth went past the table and stools to the cabinets. Unlike the other furniture in the kitchen, the cabinets were adorned: fruit and wheatears carved in the wood. Fresh, ripe food. Even with the little he knew about wizards, that looked promising. As long as the food needed no cooking.

"That route, the wizard might not have approved of," he said. "She might even have kicked us out without a meal."

He pulled the cabinet door open. It moved stiffly, if silently, and behind it, the shelves were almost empty. His eyebrows went up. Perhaps wizards were less concerned about the flesh, but then—would she not have enchanted it to fill up, so she did not have to concern herself?

He crouched to survey all the shelves. Some dried-out fruit, and an ancient loaf of bread, sat on the lowest shelf.

"What have we got?" said Perriel, turning from the window, and her gaze fell on the cabinet. For a moment, she did not seem even to breathe. Then she strode over, half-closed the doors to study the carvings, and yanked them open. Her breath came so lightly and so quickly that he swallowed. She must have recognized the cabinet, and she had not expected this.

Perriel poked the bread, and it crumbled into dust. Her expression went through several variants of disbelief. She touched the fruit, gently, with her finger; then she jabbed it. It did not crumble—or move.

After a moment, she swept away the remnants of the bread. She eyed the shelf as if expecting nothing to happen—as if she checked that another loaf would not appear.

"That wizard can't eat here," said Gareth. "No one could."

"She can not eat here." Perriel's voice sounded as remote as a frost fairy's, and she had turned as pale as one. She turned to face him. "I told you that wizards can forget everything in their studies."

"She can't forget to eat!" Then, more weakly, he added, "She'd die."

Perriel looked back at the cabinet. "Wizards deep in study can ignore *everything* else."

"They can't ignore...."

His throat choked on the word. He could not say that they could not ignore death—and he did not need to. Perriel would assure him that they could.

He could not speak. It was hard to breathe.

And the wizard had even offered to help them!

"Are we in danger?" he said.

Her voice was clipped, precise, as if she recited a lesson. She did not glance away from the cabinet. "Whatever its intentions toward us, a ghost is dangerous to all life. To have broken the spell on this—" She tapped the cabinet. "—required a great deal of death. The stone outside may not be Zavrien's work. She might have blighted the grass from the ground." Her gaze darted toward the window. "I helped once, restore land a ghost had blighted. As a prentice, but it took many spells."

She turned to face him. "If we stay here, she will sap the life out of us." Her voice lowered. "She seems fascinated enough with the curse that she would not let us leave."

Interest, thought Gareth bitterly.

"We could try to escape." Perriel bit her lower lip. "If she tries to stop us—it might not be too difficult to stop her. Her ghostly life comes from her not having noticed. We would have to make her notice." She drew in a deep breath and let it out again. "It takes time for a ghost to fade. The more she sees that proves it, the swifter it will happen. But even as a ghost fades, it can cast spells."

Gareth felt his face set into a bitter mask. He had let Perriel convince him that the curse might be broken. He should have known better.

"We can see if we can get out the window," said Perriel. She started to turn toward it.

The wizard's voice echoed in the stairway. "Have you eaten?"

Before Perriel could move, the wizard finished descending. Her feet touching the stone made no sound. How could they—how could *she*—have missed that, when their footsteps had clattered and resounded? Gareth swallowed. He was not even certain that she cast a shadow.

Then the wizard stood in the kitchen. "Have you?"

"No," said Perriel, stepping from the cabinet. Gareth pulled back, unwilling to even stand close as the wizard glided across the floor, though the air did not feel cold, or dry, or dead, from her

passing. He swallowed again. Was she walking? Or did she think
of moving, without noticing that she had no legs?

"Was something wrong?" the wizard said, drifting toward
them. "I have always found the food sustaining."

"When you ate," Perriel said, heavily.

The wizard looked at her sleeves and raised her hands. The
sleeves fell back from the wizard's hands: graceful, strong, bone-
white—translucent.

Gareth retreated, aware that soon his back would reach the
wall. His foot scrapped on the stone.

The wizard raised her head at the noise. The hood fell back
from the face of a middle-aged woman, her expression contorted
with fury into inhuman lines. "Why did you come to plague me?
I curse you! I curse you!" Her voice grew less human with every
word, taking on harshness like a crow's. "I curse you! May your
path be forever a maze to you! May. . . ."

Gareth lunged at her. His arms went through cloth and body
as if nothing was there. He staggered through a patch of icy air,
colder than he had ever faced in Zavrien's lands, and his blood
felt congealed in his veins. He collapsed against the wall, his
hand taking his weight.

The wizard looked over her shoulder. Her face was a shadow
on the air; it contorted with hatred and was gone.

"That," said Perriel, her voice a croak, "was wise. It proved to
her that she no longer lived." Almost as pale as the wizard, Perriel
hugged herself.

He felt as if he would never be warm again. "Did she. . ."
Gareth picked his words with care. "Did she curse us?"

"Oh yes." Her arms tightened, spasmodically. "A curse of
bewilderment. On the principles of the mapping spells, at that. I
could lay it myself, though hers is stronger. Wherever place we
try to go, we will not get there." After a moment, she added,
"Much stronger. I have no hopes of breaking it."

I should have left Perriel, Gareth thought. No promise could justify dragging her into this. The thought weighed on his soul like lead. "It's all over, then."

"Probably." Her voice was light, flat, matter of fact. She did not look at him.

He could not explain the weight her words added to his heart.

She glanced at where the ghost had dissolved. "On the other hand," she said, her voice desperately cheerful, "we have the wizard's books. I can read them. So can you—I heard the army teaches the infant oblates to read. . . ."

"I won't know what to look for."

"Spell-breaking," said Perriel. "Anything and everything about breaking spells. Then I can see if it's useful."

"You are the wizard. The army found you master enough of spells to hire you. I—"

Perriel laughed, harshly. "Because of my mastery of spells of motion." She gestured at the cabinet. The door slammed shut, sending a gust across the room. "Not bewilderment. Not weather magic. Not disenchanting. Certainly not curses. No wizard knows everything—and if I tried too hard, I could have turned out like *her*." Her mouth set. "Not that I had much chance, after my master— died."

Gareth looked at her with narrowed eyes.

Perriel said, her voice brittle, "He was a diabolist. One day Cory and I came early for our lessons and caught him at it. We denounced him before he could do something like *that*." She gestured at the snow outside. "They executed him, but no wizard would take us as prentices, so we had to let the army hire us."

After a silent minute, Gareth said, "Your parents?"

"After they had already paid my prentice fee?" Perriel snorted. "I could support myself; they would not pay twice."

Her shoulders hunched as she looked away. She did not even glance at the stairs, and Gareth had never seen her look so defeated. He scrambled for anything to say.

"If she had no food here—do we have enough supplies?"

Perriel frowned in thought. "If this *did* work. . . ." She walked over to the cabinet. "I could not make it, but perhaps I could restore it. She might have had spells that would warm the tower as well, and fetch water." Her face lit up with a smile. "Then we could hunt long and long for spell-breaking. You might even learn to cast the spell yourself."

If I didn't bring the tower down on us, thought Gareth, but his relief at her good cheer kept the words behind his mouth. Perriel was not herself when she did not think they would survive.

She dropped her pack on the table. "Not so hungry that I want to eat our supplies early, and I do not want to drag it up and down the stairs."

Gareth thought of trekking those stairs every time they wanted to eat. "We could leave the food upstairs, and eat without leaving the books."

"Crumbs attract mice."

Gareth glanced at the waste outside. After a moment, a pink-cheeked Perriel said, "We might spill things on the books—and it's a *bad habit*. You don't want to get into bad habits."

As if they were likely to suffer from their accumulation!

"Besides, you want to move after you have read for a long time. You get stiff—and it is a harbinger of worse things." She scowled at the floor. "We should sleep down here, too."

The worse things would not have time to arrive, but Gareth peeled off his pack. She might be right about stiffness. And Perriel started back up the stairs.

She stopped at the first door. "If she had studied breaking spells and lost interest, she might have stored. . . ."

She shoved on the door. It slid open without a sound, though the cold air smelled musty. A pleasant room, beneath the dust, spread before them: wardrobe in one corner, a fireplace in one wall, a great bed opposite it. Perriel studied it intently.

Gareth scowled. "Something is wrong here."

"You remembered how tight the stairway was," Perriel said. "This room is too large. It would not fit in the tower."

Gareth looked uneasily at the room.

"A *very* powerful wizard indeed," said Perriel, brightly, pulling shut the door. "There is hope!"

In the kitchen, Perriel sat with a tome in her lap. The wizard's crabbed handwriting had not been easy to pick out from the rest of the works, many of which were equally hard to read, but she had found the right book. She trusted.

Gareth stood by the stairway—a dark, silent, *watching* shadow. She considered the cabinet again. Fruit and bread would prove a meager diet, but she did not want to try generating food that the wizard had not done before. Not when Gareth would take anything going wrong as proof of the curse's dreadful power.

"I thought wizards could not create anything," said Gareth.

"We don't," said Perriel.

"So this steals?"

He *had* listened.

"No. It *transforms*. An apple tree can make more apples from sunlight, earth, air, and water. This can do the same."

"All these spells work like that?" said Gareth. "None of them steal?"

"No," said Perriel more sharply, "but I've read her notes." She shifted the book into better light. "And thieving cabinets draw the attention of the army. Which would distract the wizard from her work."

She read the freshening spell again. Gareth shifted his weight.

"For what I am doing—freshening the spell—only contagion effects are needed," said Perriel. "Thing that are in contact continue to affect each other after they are out of contact. I have to draw them back together. You can refresh just about any enchanted thing that way, even if you can not fathom the original spell."

Gareth looked lost in thought. Perriel smiled. She might make a wizard of him yet. She intoned the words.

Moments later, the very air felt different. She closed the book. Gareth strode past her to open the cabinets. Fruit—not dried, but fresh—sprung up on two shelves, and a third had bread. Perriel's mouth watered: peaches, grapes, plums, apples, strawberries, and still more fruit, not all of which she could identify. She grabbed a plum and bit into its tangy pulp. She licked her lips to snag the juice. The wizard had not stinted on the spell; all the stranger, that she had forgotten to eat. Unless the spell had been only practice to her.

Perriel got down to the pit. The more fool the wizard. Gareth still stared at the cabinet, until, with a scowl, he pulled open the next cabinet: dried meat, and cheese.

Perriel finally found her voice and said, "With magefire to melt the snow, we can look as long as we need to, to find some way to break these curses."

She picked a hunk of cheese up. "She must have been a ghost long and long; that was a sturdy spell and would not have broken in a month or two of her not noticing it." She bit into the cheese, far fresher than the army's, chewed, and swallowed. "We should eat well. We need to keep up our strength for the hunt through the books."

Perriel would be safe here.

She did not need winter lore to survive in the Golden Tower, and so his promise was void. She could melt snow for water, she had plentiful food, better than the army had, and the tower would shelter her from the winter.

Gareth leaned from the window. The chill of early morning made him shiver. Which was to say, she would be safe if misfortune did not plague her. If he left, Winter's Curse would wear off. It took time, but better that than rummaging through all those books that *might* have the knowledge to break the curse. Even the master wizard, with years more knowledge than Perriel, had admitted she would have to search.

Perriel had been hopeful when she declared that they could have gotten in through the window, but out was another matter. The snow was deep enough to break his fall.

He dropped his pack into the snow. He had taken all the army supplies, and as much of the food from the cabinet as he would eat before it spoiled; that would help appease Perriel. He slung his legs over the window's edge and dropped himself.

Snow sprang through every gap to worm its way under his clothing, sometimes to his bare skin. Gareth gasped. He sat up, shed as much snow as he could, and grabbed his pack. He might even seek out this Spell-Breaker that Perriel had spoken of.

First, he had to escape the Golden Tower and Perriel. He slung on the pack and eyed the landscape. The eastern sky was pale yellow with dawn. He could travel far today, and all he had to do was get away.

The wind made the snow hiss over itself, the fine grains already blurring the edges of where he fell. It would worm its way under his hood, through the lacings of his cloak.

Perriel would say that he should walk with his back to it.

Grimacing at the thought, but unable to say why, Gareth walked away.

Perriel looked up from a stack of books. Morning light spread from the window over the room, revealing row on row of books—the sun had risen high enough that it did not shine directly through the window—and no sign of Gareth. She scowled and shoved back her chair. He did not think their escape likely, but what sort of excuse was that to dawdle over a meal? She stalked down the stairs to the kitchen, where their cots stood.

The kitchen stood empty.

The window stood open a crack, and a chilly draft drifted over the floor despite the spells. Perriel, feeling as numb as if the cold had frozen her, walked over. Beneath, the wind-swept snow showed dips and rises, but no tracks.

Perriel dragged in her breath and, to be sure, climbed the stairs, testing each door and finding the dust behind untroubled, until she reached the top, without a sign of Gareth. She looked uneasily about. She was not the new wizard of the Golden Tower, she was not *that* lost in her studies, she would have heard Gareth returning.

Carefully, she looked about the room. Then she inspected each corner where Gareth might have hidden from view. Biting her lip, she crept down the stairs again: she had not ransacked the kitchens for hiding places.

She peered up the chimney, but that was clear, and then looked about. Beneath the stairway stood another door. Her heart hammered. If Gareth had noticed it, and gone in—she had not thought there might be other dangers, believing the ghost's presence would have dealt with *them* as well. But there could be dangers in a wizard's tower that did not leave.

Oddly enough, the door opened to a small corridor, leading under the stairs, as if nothing else would fit. Perriel summoned up the magefire to glow over her shoulder, and walked inside. Another room appeared before her. With tubs and screens, and pumps for water. Perriel stared at it. One thought intruded: no more need to melt snow for water. She shook her head, and another thought succeeded that one: she itched for the want of bathing, her hair was filthy, and her clothing she had worn for weeks.

If Gareth had found it, he might have washed himself, but then he would have told her.

Perriel stalked from the room. Gareth did not hide there. It was like trying to lean on a wall, only to find it a glamour, and staggering without a bit of balance.

Outside, the wind bore a veil of fine snow. How long had Gareth been gone? How hard had the wind blown? Enough to cover his tracks?

How *could* he? Perriel buried her face in her hands. He had promised—he had—but only not to abandon her in the winter wilds. She felt herself shaking and could not even try to stop it. He suffered under two curses now, and he had thought one was reason enough to give up hope.

Gareth must have thought to save her by losing himself, she realized.

She let out her breath very slowly. The dear, sweet *idiot*.

She shook her head. She must not—that would do Gareth no good, and someone had to think of his well-bring. She thought of the tracks again, and ran over the books she had been reading. One had mentioned of a far-seeing spell. It would let her find Gareth at least.

She bolted for the stairs. Ever-living and all-merciful God, let her find Gareth and save the fool from freezing to death. "Lord have mercy, Christ have mercy, Lord have mercy. St. Casper, pray for me. St. Melchior, pray for me. St. Balthazar, pray for me."

The sky was colorful again, this time with fiery red and vivid gold. His pack weighed on his shoulders; it had not felt that heavy when he and Perriel arrived at the Golden Tower. Gareth sighed. It had been a troublesome day. The baffling contortions of hills had not made it easy to find his way.

Perriel would inquire why, if it did not matter where he was going, it mattered so much if he could tell his way. He could almost see her asking it, bright-eyed and smiling.

Gareth groaned and plodded about the hill. There, on a slope covered with loose rock, stood a tower, golden in the sunset—or rather, more golden in the sunset. Gareth stopped. He could see the window. If Perriel stood at it, she could see him.

His shoulders slumped. Finally, he turned away, hoping that being this close would not affect Perriel again.

He collided with something. Nothing was there, he could see the snow before him, but he put forth his hand, and ran it over a wall, as transparent as air, and far harder to advance against than the wind.

Perriel's voice carried over the snow. "Don't even try."

He looked back. During the moment he had turned away, she had appeared in the window. Thin as it had sounded, her voice could not carry that far.

Then, she was a wizard.

She leaned out of the window, and spoke as if she stood next to him. "I won't let you. If you try, you will make me waste even more time than you already have."

Gareth's hands clenched into fists.

"*She* cursed you, too. Didn't you listen? Our journeys will be mazes; we will be unable to go where we wish—until we break that one as well. Winter's Curse takes precedence, as more dangerous."

Slowly, Gareth forced his hands to relax. He walked toward her, and Perriel, without a word, pulled back into the tower but watched his every step. At the foot of the tower, he looked at her, for some reason certain that she, and not Corry, had determined that they had to denounce their master for his diabolerie.

He felt ready to weep. All the effort had gone to nothing.

"How do you intend to get me up there?" he said.

Perriel felt light-headed. "Stand there." Her tongue touched her lip. She did not want to have the spell falter and give Gareth a moment to reconsider. She had lifted things with the shield spell before, but it was tricky, and none of them had been easy to damage, or hard to replace. And she had not had giddy thoughts haunting her with the knowledge that he was alive, he was well, he was back. . . .

She drew a deep breath before she cast it.

Gareth rose so smoothly that she had to scramble out of the way, to let him in the window. He stepped in—alive, intact, uninjured, moving without any hesitation and showing no signs of bruises, or even cold. For a moment, after shutting the window, Perriel just stood and watched him. He took off his pack and coat as easily, as well.

Gareth would have a hard time explaining why *this* was a manifestation of the curse, but she felt so gleeful that she did not point that out, only danced across the floor and yanked open the door.

"Look. Baths."

Gareth looked as if he were about to waver. Then he said, slowly, "Aren't there magical creatures that live in springs?"

"*Live*, Gareth, *live*. No matter how magical they are, the ghost's presence would have killed them years ago." She stepped inside and grinned. "There's even soap. A ghost did not affect *that*. And, of course, there's no way to heat the water because a wizard needs only magefire."

Her grin deepened. Perhaps she should see if there were any spells to conjure up clothing. Then they would have all that they needed.

His absence had done her no harm, but Perriel in her elation looked more like a princess rescued from the dragon's maw than a maiden under a deadly curse.

"Food, first," he said.

After a moment, she shrugged. "Certainly let us eat," she said, half-laughing. "A feast to celebrate the safe return of the traveler."

Her eyes were bright. Her braids had not quite kept her hair subdued; strands formed an aura about the braids, and he found himself wondering what she would look like clean, well clad, and unharried.

The sounds of water filling the tub and of cloth being shed reminded her that he was on the other side of the screen. Gareth had lit his bath with his own magefire; the red glow was invisible, except where reflected from the ceiling. She forced her gaze away.

She kept her own violet-blue light low. The water surface, choppy from the water flowing in, reflect a pattern of black and violet.

She shed her clothing, slid within, and let the warmth ease about her. She tugged at her hair, at the braid that she had done and undone, but had never properly combed out in the wilderness. Wet and free, it swam about her like a mermaid's— though it would be like damp seaweed once she got out.

She reached for her comb. The sounds from the other side of the screen showed that Gareth was climbing into his bath. She set about applying soap and comb to her hair. He had been foolish indeed, leaving like that, but now, giddy with his safe return, she would concede that the fool had done it with the sincere desire to protect her.

She snorted. As if a maid who had denounced her own master for his diabolerie needed much in the way of protection. She swept her hair about the water to rinse it out.

Gareth must have wanted only to get away from the Golden Tower. If he tried to reach another place, such as the Spell-Breaker's lands, he would have missed it, but he might, instead of circling round, have made it to a third place. She chuckled. She would not mention that flaw to him, but that he had not noticed was enough to show that Winter's Curse was not a death sentence. They had a chance.

She reached for the soap again, and grabbed it too tightly. It leapt, slippery, from her fingers, out of the tub, and clattered on the floor. Silence came from the other side, making her keenly aware of the noises that had ended. Her mouth twisted. Nothing like clumsiness to show how competent she was to look after herself. She clambered out—and her wet foot missed the step, and slid out.

She cried out in surprise, until the flagstones knocked the breath out of her.

Gareth called, sharply, "Are you all right?"

She should speak, tell him that she was all right. . . but dragging down a breath did not give her the power of speech.

Water sloshed on the other side, his footsteps sounded on the floor, and his bare hand touched her arm.

"Are you all right?"

She felt a fool. She pushed off the stone, rising to her knees. "I just fell; I'm not hurt. Bruised, maybe."

Gareth glanced at them, and she became keenly aware of their nakedness. She glanced at him, and glanced away, but her mouth still felt bone-dry. He had, indeed, suffered no injuries from his foolish journey—at least that she could see.

He dropped to one knee beside her. Despite his folly, he was back, alive and well. Her hand went out, almost without her willing it, to brush against the warmth of his arm and be sure of it.

Even beneath her tentative fingers, she felt the muscle flex beneath the skin. Gareth leaned forward. His mouth brushed hers. Alive indeed. She leaned forward to return the kiss, and put her arms about his shoulders.

The next morning, the sky was bright and clear and blue, without a cloud to be seen anywhere over the wind-swept snow. That showed no signs of Gareth's venture.

Perriel stood in the wizard's library. Though it was midmorning, and she had seen no sign of Gareth, she felt not the slightest impulse to search for him. Her body ached, and the thought made her flush.

She had been a fool —an utter fool. Even in her relief and delight that he was alive.

Her hand went over the books again. One, strangely written, was marked Simples. Perriel opened it and flipped through the pages: simples indeed, common spells that any cunning woman might know, for burns and beestings, for fertility in man or beast, and more. "A spell for sowing seeds over land—what's wrong with doing it by hand?" Perriel muttered.

She read the next, and her finger stopped as if captured. Breathing hard, Perriel read it again. For whether a woman carried a child.

She stood by the shelf a long minute. Then she yanked the book over to the table, sat, and studied.

The spell was not difficult; it took her less time than was quite pleasant to attempt it. Her heart hammering, she cast it. A soft green glow appeared between her hands, a rounded oval. Perriel cupped it between her fingers, as if it were a fragile bird's egg that she had to protect, though the green cloud, brushing her fingers, could not be felt, only seen.

She swallowed. The shades of green shifted. Green within the light, taking shape within the heart of the glow. It shifted again.

She stared in disbelief. It was, indeed, two shapes. As if one were not enough.

Her heart threw itself against her chest in its hammering. She was a fool. Thrice a fool. Gareth had told her how dangerous the curse was, again and again. First she had ignored him, and then, in her giddiness, she had acted as if she had already broken the spell. Not remembering that it lay, lurking, ready to turn folly into disaster—into their bringing the curse on an innocent child. Or rather, children.

She wished she could weep. But her eyes felt bone dry.

"Lord, have mercy," she whispered. "Christ, have mercy. Lord, have mercy. St. Michael, Archangel, pray for us." She could not think for a moment. "Holy Innocents, pray for us."

She heard footsteps on the stairs. They were slow.

Perriel sat, her hands covering her face, when he reached the tower top. Gareth squared his shoulders. If she had known what they did, so had he. He had to own his own share of the folly.

She had, he noted, braided her hair again, severely. He stepped inside the door.

She lowered her hands, and he felt queasy. She did not look ready to rail at him, but she looked more distressed than he had believed possible.

A book lay open before her. She slammed it shut. Her cheeks colored, to an unbecoming red. "I came with child."

For a long minute, the words made no sense at all. Then Gareth looked away before she could watch his face heat. His hand clenched into a fist. He should have foreseen that. Perriel had never believed the threat of the curse, and he had. He should have known the curse would find a way to worsen their plight.

"Twins," she added.

He could imagine no words of comfort, and she looked as if saying anything would break her control.

Perriel rose. Her gaze flickered past Gareth toward the books. She walked to them, but her fingers drifted over them rather than pulling any out.

He did not much want to study himself, but however desultory their reading was, it would have more hope—such as it was—than moping about. He walked up to the books, a section far from Perriel's, but the names on the bindings signified nothing to him.

"If you dismiss a book," said Perriel, dully, without looking up, "put it aside, just as if you though I should look at it. So that we do not look at books twice."

She put a book aside, off the shelf.

His arms ached. From stretching for books, from lugging them about, from standing while hunting through them—he should have sat to read, and not stood wherever he was, but if they had any hope at all, it lay in speed. He looked up from the latest tome.

The sun was setting. Gareth blinked and looked at. Setting. And not just having turned all the sunlight golden or orange. The sun set in masses of scarlet and crimson—in clouds that had also arisen without his noticing.

He lowered the book. So this was how the wizards managed to forget all in their studies.

He walked over to the empty shelf and put a book in it. This one would be ones they had dismissed. Perriel raised her hands to gesture for the magefire, and violet-blue light filled the tower room. Gareth looked at her face for a minute, comparing to soldiers who had made forced marches. Some of it might be the color the light shed, but. . . .

Besides, Perriel had never had to endure such marches. And she was with child.

"You have eat," said Gareth. The harshness of his voice surprised him, but he could not stop. "And sleep."

"I have to find a way to break the curse," said Perriel.

"You have to consider your health," said Gareth. When she opened her mouth again, he glanced at her waist.

Perriel clapped shut both her mouth and the book. In this light, he could not be sure she blushed.

Days of searching.

It would take weeks before they could declare they had searched everything, but Gareth could see that looming ahead.

God help them both, they had to discover something to free themselves. His fingers ran over the books, and he pulled one out at random. Not one showing many signs of use. Gareth flipped it open. His gaze went over pages of prayers, and readings from scripture. No wonder the wizard had not used it much; its mere presence surprised him. He fanned several pages, wondering if it contained a prayer service for times of distress. One appeared.

He tried to collect his thoughts and read, "Nothing has befallen you save what is common to man."

Gareth froze. The words echoed and re-echoed in his mind. "Save what is common to man." His thoughts ran back over the last weeks. God help me, he thought, desperately.

"Gareth?" said Perriel, with more than a touch of sharpness. Her hands were full of a book, but if he had realized the truth, that was more important.

"What happened to the wizard of the Golden Tower—that has happened to other wizards, often?" he asked.

Perriel's eyebrows shot up. After a minute, she said, "Not often, but it happens. It happened to one near my master's tower. I helped restore the lands he had blighted."

He could not find words to speak.

"I suppose it would be more likely here, where wizards did not care to flee the winter." Her mouth twisted. "We care. We are not in that danger."

Gareth shook his head, trying to clear it. The frost fairies had found Perriel in the manner they had all been warned against.

"What if there was no curse?" he said, his voice barely a croak.

Perriel opened her mouth and shut it again. Then she blinked, like an owlet in noon sunlight, and stared at him. "Everyone—*you* said it was—"

"What if Zavrien said there was, and let all our ill luck be blamed on it?"

She blinked again.

"They blamed the army's defeat on us, and Zavrien already knew where they were. He was bound to attack."

Color drained from Perriel's face. "We've had—other problems."

"Nothing that can't befall someone in the winter lands."

"That would be. . ." She picked her next word slowly. "*Fiendish.*" Her hand went to her mouth. "Most of our misery has come from the army's exiling us."

His heart hammered so loudly that he was surprised it did not echo. He forced his breath out, and his thoughts roiled.

"It can't be true. Someone would have guessed by now," he whispered. "How many soldiers has he cursed?"

"How long have they lasted after?" Perriel said. She clung to her book if it were a shield. "When the army drove them off, into Zavrien's lands?" She frowned for a moment and said, sharply. "Did they cast them out from the very beginning?"

"The army has suffered defeats at Zavrien's hands. Once he had cast his forces against them, and let them blame it on the curse, they would have a reason to believe it."

Her hand went to her waist.

"Women have come with child without a curse," Gareth said. Perriel blushed. He gentled his voice. "Misfortune happens, but once Zavrien had told us all that the curse existed, we all blamed every misfortune on it."

Gareth put the book back, with care. It could not be.

"Has he ever cursed a wizard?" said Perriel.

Gareth racked his memory. "No, he has not."

Slowly, she nodded. "A wizard could watch him cast the spell and recognize it as an illusion, not a curse. And that would explain why the illusion hid the curse so perfectly." Her breath came light and fast. "I can break illusions."

Perriel puttered around for an hour after, with glasses and powders. Sunset faded, and magefire gave their only light, instead. Silvery and ruddy dust stained her fingers, and she muttered under her breath. Gareth leaned against the wall, unable to relax. If he had guessed wrong. . . his thoughts trailed off, unable to guess about consequences. A handful of spells did not make him a wizard.

"Stand there, Gareth." Perriel pointed, and Gareth walked over. She chanted in a clear high voice—a short spell—and clapped the book shut again.

"That does that. A simple spell indeed. That it broke so easily is proof that there was nothing more behind it."

Gareth tried to look down, at his cheek. The mark had never been more than a suggestion of black in the corner of his sight. Only by straining could he see that it was gone.

"I suppose," said Perriel, dryly, "that we should tell the army the secret."

Gareth said, even more dryly, "The wizard of the Golden Tower laid another curse on us. Is that one also an illusion?"

Perriel threw one hand in the air. "So I will break that one. Food, water, shelter—books!—are all to be found here, so her curse will not kill us, but we will have to escape sometime. Or at least, we will want to."

Gareth felt a cold draft but dismissed it. He glanced at her waist. "Good. I do not think that a priest will wander this far in time."

Perriel turned pink. Gareth closed the distance between them to kiss her. She turned even more pink, and did not meet his gaze, but went on, doggedly, "The confusion spell is not the Winter's Curse—nothing more than an illusion."

"Oh," said another voice, familiar, from the hallway, "there was something more to it."

Gareth felt his blood congeal. He stepped away from Perriel. She looked at the doorway and back to Gareth. Without looking, he nodded. Then he faced Zavrien.

The wizard walked in. His black robes, embroidered with coppery runes, swirled about him. The air chilled. Gareth shivered. It was not merely terror on his part; it grew colder. He glanced through the doorway. Zavrien had brought none of his creatures with him. Then, he could dispose of a half-trained wizard, and a soldier with not a dozen spells, by himself.

"I watch that spell," said Zavrien. "No one will tell the army of their own wickedness, inspired by no more than a trick on my part."

"You inflicted this on us," said Perriel, "and you call it a *trick*!"

Zavrien's lip curled. "If the army can not realize what I did, if they are such cowards, and such knaves that they abuse me for wickedness when they treacherously abandon their own, they do not deserve to know. And you will not tell them."

"*Deserve*," said Gareth.

"I had assailed them with my loyal forces before. But when I marked one of their company, they were ready to blame him. And I never had to assail them again." Zavrien glanced between them and lifted an eyebrow. "I have only watched the spell, not you. I do not know what has befallen you; I sent nothing after you. You fathomed the spell, so you know that the army inflicted the misery. They have no right to call me wicked."

"No right?" Gareth's voice cracked.

Zavrien whirled on him. "What have I done that others have not? It was *their* treachery that sent me to that—unfortunate spell, and *they* meant to do it." His eyes were large as he stared at Gareth.

That was why he talked when he laid the curse, Gareth realized; he was trying to convince me, or himself, that it was justified.

"Since then, I have only defended myself."

Gareth remembered the skeletons in the snow and felt mute.

"Your lands have spread," spat Perriel.

"What else am I to do? Permit the army to murder me? The same army that abandoned you to your deaths?"

"Says the wizard who intends to murder us," said Gareth.

"*Intends*?" said Zavrien. "I do not *intend*. You invaded my land, and I will have my rights. That it will prevent you from tale-bearing is also good."

Perriel braced herself. Her voice was belligerent. "You should not have left your citadel, where you are strongest."

Zavrien raised his hand. White lightning lashed out and thundered in the tiny room. Perriel threw up both her hands, drawing the lightning into them; she caught every lash, her hands darting about like minnows in a river, but she strained to do it. Zavrien smiled, more deeply, and raised his other hand. Quickly he threw it toward Gareth. Gareth lunged forward, and into a wall of air, like the one Perriel had conjured.

Zavrien, looking smug, turned his back on him.

Gareth fought to steady his breath as Perriel caught Zavrien's lightnings. He would murder her, and the babies, and then he would dispose of the soldier, who—

Zavrien had never cursed a wizard. Gareth dragged in a deep breath. Zavrien must have ensured that he was not a wizard before sending the frost fairy and giant after him. And Zavrien had bragged of not watching them since he had laid the curse.

Which meant he did not know that Gareth *was* a wizard now. So to speak.

Gareth sidled against the wall, to ensure that he stood behind Zavrien, where no stray glance would reveal his actions. He wished for Perriel's lightless spell, where no shadow would reveal his magefire before the heat acted, but he had no time to waste on regrets.

Narrowing his eyes, he summoned magefire, blazing ruby red, and as close to Zavrien as he could conjure it. The light flared behind Zavrien; Gareth could feel the heat through the air. He pushed it forward, against Zavrien's robes. In moments, the cloth smoldered.

Gareth's heart beat, once, twice—Zavrien cried out. As if that was an order, his robes flamed. He jerked his head around, trying to peer over his shoulder.

Perriel lifted her hands, still filled with lightnings, and hurled them back. The air crackled and gleamed, and Zavrien screamed in pain. Perriel's hand rose to conjure magefire, and Zavrien's robes exploded into fire.

Zavrien screamed, loud and piercing. He staggered, and Gareth wondered what else he could set ablaze—and he was going toward Perriel.

Perriel's hands leapt through the air. Zavrien collided with her wall of air. Snarling, he clawed the air toward Gareth, and hit his own wall of air. His mouth opened again, but no shout came out. He glared at Gareth, his eyes frothing with the same hatred as when he complained of the injustice he had suffered—and then the fire leapt, and his charred body collapsed against the wall, to slide to the floor. There it lay, and burned, until it sank to smoldering.

The air stank of its smoke.

Perriel said, her voice high and light, "I didn't think that we had a chance."

Gareth said, "May God have mercy on his soul." He could get little hope into his voice, after the hatred that had contorted Zavrien in his last moments—but the man was dead. He steadied his breath.

Perriel's hands went up in a spell. After a moment, he recognized the coffin spell, even before she had conjured up the box that took in the remains—down to the ghastly smoke. Then, they had to be rid of the body. He let his breath out slowly.

Something splashed, outside. He looked at the window. Water dripped from the roof. And then a chunk of ice and snow pulled loose and plummeted.

He pushed open the window. Even in the night, warm air blew in.

"I suppose," Perriel said, lightly, distantly, "that his spells were of the manner that work only for his lifetime."

She stared out as if seeing nothing, as if trying to drink in what had happened. Slowly, a smile crept onto her face, and broadened, brighter than the dawn. She came up beside him, and cast a magefire out the window—not so warm, but brilliantly white and gold. As far as they could see, snow melted and streamed. Already bare earth showed here and there, and the patches widened as they watched.

Long minutes later, Perriel dropped the spell. "It won't finish in a moment," she said. "We should go rest, and see what the morning brings."

Gareth nodded. "We have much to consider then."

Perriel rose before he did. For a moment, his arm thrown across his face, Gareth considered going back to sleep, but her feet padded across the floor to the window, and did not stir from it, and—who knew what lay outside?

The sky was delicate pinks and creams, and beneath, the hills showed a patchwork of brown and white—white mostly in the sheltered nooks—and streams and ponds of water.

"How good for us," said Perriel, lightly. "Life is hard enough when you do not finish your apprenticeship, and you can't join the army." She turned to face him. "I do not want to give up this tower. We can study wizardry, and no doubt we will not be alone."

Gareth let out his breath. "You said that you had to help restore the land—where the wizard had died. What with the winter, I do not think Zavrien's lands will be hale. About here, there was the ghost, as well."

Perriel nodded. "I will study how to break the other curse. You will study to restore it. I did the restoration while an apprentice." Then she smiled. "And I saw a spell to cast seed over the land. We could turn it to green easily enough."

It was still dawn, the hills dark, the clouds showing shades of dark gray. Gareth looked down at the rousing town. Perriel had insisted on landing outside it, and actually walking within, but their magical arrival had been noted—and perhaps, so had the direction they had come from.

Her fingers linked with his. The crowds gathered as they walked.

"You!" called a lanky man, his face hard. Perriel's fingers tightened on Gareth's. "You know what happened *there*!" He gestured at the hills. Where the snow had been. Where green just sprouted, here and there, and yellowy with newness.

"You must, you must," said a plump woman, breathlessly. "You came from there—"

Faces full of hope and wonder and questions turned toward them. Even the youngest among them looked worn.

Perriel let out her breath. "Zavrien is dead," she called, loudly enough to heard throughout the crowd. "His spells have broken."

Gasps of surprise surrounded them, and soon a crowd. One young woman said, "It would be *safe* to live there?"

"We're living there," said Gareth.

"You're wizards," said a small girl, and in her mouth, it sounded like an accusation.

He felt keenly aware of the book he had brought with him in case he had a moment to study: *Simples*, for its curative spells. He still studied the most basic ones, and hoped to reach those to aid a woman in childbirth in time. But he could cast spells.

"That is how we know that wizardry has made the land green and pleasant, enough for others to live there as well—"

"What are you doing *here*?" said an old woman, suspiciously.

"Marrying," said Gareth. His hand tightened on Perriel's. "Before the church door and witnesses."

Their efforts had turned the hills green, but they had not restored the woods that had grown before. Even now, the slopes showed only saplings.

The town of Golden Tower had, therefore, risen up in buildings of stone, as it grew up about the foot of the tower, as peasants and merchants and tradesmen flocked to the land. Where better than where two wizards already lived—wizards from whom spells could be purchased?

Perriel smiled wryly. She and Gareth had barely fenced off enough ground for a stairway, and a garden, before the town engulfed them. They had mastered the spells to add space within the tower; they had needed to.

Elena and Kenelm, solemn as judges, weeded their corner of the garden. The younger children, squealing with glee, ran across the grass to bounce off the spell to keep them from trampling the plots—and then ran back to bounce again.

She smiled a little. They would have to add space to the garden, too, and soon.

A voice outside carried, farther perhaps than intended: "A wizard named Perriel was with General Ryna's army, but the other wizard was Corry."

She glanced at Gareth. He must have heard; he looked up from the desk.

"Still," said another soldier, "even if not that Perriel, they could help fight diabolerie. The townsfolk speak highly of their magic."

A breeze blew in the window, rustling papers.

"We could pretend we're not here," Perriel said in a low voice.

"They'll come back," said Gareth, marking his place. "The army needs wizards. It needs them very much." His mouth twitched. "They took you and Cory on. That was not kindness for two prentices who had done their duty."

The heavy clatter of the knocker resounded. Perriel sighed and turned from the window. Adding rooms to the tower had added stairs to it as well, but it still took less time than she liked to reach the door.

The captain and soldiers bowed with overt respect, but she felt cold and still.

"Good mistress, good master, we have come to appeal for your aid. Your wizardry is needed for more than the simples you provide for this town."

Perriel swallowed.

Gareth greeted them and escorted them to the room where they talked with clients. And she could read the strain in his face as he did it, and still more when they talked of the army's need for wizards as powerful as they were.

"Such powers are needed against evil wizards," said the captain.

"And their works," said Perriel. "There are still *-leagues* where the depredations of Zavrien mark the land—even with all our labors, even after his death."

One soldier shifted uneasily. "Is Zavrien dead?"

Perriel hesitated. They had told the villagers, she reminded herself.

"Why else would his enchantments have failed as they did? But if he is not dead, wizards are needed here to guard against his return."

"If his enchantments failed," said the captain, "he is too weak to be any danger anymore."

"His spells still taint the land." She added, firmly, "Our magic is needed here."

"That is work that any prentice could do," said the soldier.

"If it is so easy," said Perriel, "we would have been done by now." She smiled. "Besides, we have to look after the children."

Also by Mary Catelli

Curses And Wonders
Dragon Slayer
Eyes of the Sorceress
Fever and Snow
Mermaids' Song
Sword and Shadow
The Book of Bone
Witch-Prince Ways
Dragonfire and Time
Enchantments And Dragons
Jewel of the Tiger
Over the Sea, To Me
The Dragon's Cottage
The Maze, the Manor, and the Unicorn
The White Menagerie
A Diabolical Bargain
Madeleine and the Mists
Magic And Secrets
The Lion and the Library
The Princess Goes Into The Forest
The Wolf and the Ward
The Witch-Child and the Scarlet Fleet
Treachery And Spells
Winter's Curse
Crow Curse
Free Passage
Isabelle and the Siren
Journeys And Wizardry
Lifestone

Magic of the Lost God
Never Comment On A Likeness
One Name
The Drunken Mermaids
The Turtle in the Sea of Sand
Were I You
Where There Is Smoke